Clouds of dust kicked up, temporarily blinding me as Lola reared back and raised her front hooves. I coughed and blinked my stinging eyes, gripping her reins with one hand.

Finally I felt all of Lola's feet hit the ground. I saw an ATV circling around the center of the meadow and heading back in our direction, then skidding to a stop a few feet away.

"What are you doing?" I shouted. "You almost killed us!"

Normally, I'm not the yelling kind, but my adrenaline was up and my pulse was pounding in my ears.

The driver ripped off his helmet and my breath caught in my throat. As angry as I was, I knew that I had never seen anyone this beautiful before in my life.

He's an invader, Cassie, I told myself. *Get a grip.*

Tourist Trap

EMMA HARRISON

AVON BOOKS
An Imprint of HarperCollins*Publishers*

www.harperteen.com
Library of Congress Catalog Card Number: 2005906566
ISBN-10: 0-06-084735-2
ISBN-13: 978-0-06-084735-7

Typography by Karin Paprocki
❖
First Avon edition, 2006
09 10 11 12 13 OPM 10 9 8 7 6 5 4

Tourist Trap

Chapter One

"Ladies and gentlemen! It is my privilege to present to you this year's graduating class of Lake Logan High School!"

As the entire auditorium echoed with cheers and applause, I sat back in my metal folding chair and grinned. He had said it. Old Mr. Baldetti had actually said the words I had been salivating to hear every single day since first stepping foot inside Lake Logan High. I, Cassandra Grace, was officially a graduate. My life was finally about to begin.

Of course, I had to get through the summer first, but that was all planned out. I had already signed up twice as many riding students as I normally did, hoping to earn the extra money

I would need to enter the novice jumper competition at the county fair, which was held at the end of August. Then, when I won that, I would have the $20,000 grand prize in my bank account when I started the University of Vermont in the fall—money that would be used for food, books, and fun. With all the work and training I was planning on doing, the summer would just fly by. Yes, I had a plan. Cassie Grace always had a plan.

"We did it!" my best friend, Donna Policastro, shouted as everyone shot their mortarboards in the air, then ducked and covered as they rained back down. She climbed over crouching bodies and wove around groups of hugging friends to throw her arms around my neck. She almost succeeded in tackling me to the floor. Luckily, all-state linebacker Michael Grossman broke our fall. "We did it! We graduated!"

"We are so outta here!" I exclaimed.

"Sayonara Lake Logan High!"

Donna's round face beamed and her blue eyes were wide with excitement. Her red curly hair stuck out in all directions, bobby pins hanging out at the oddest angles where she had torn off her cap.

"Adios, small town U.S.A.!" I returned.

Donna's twin brother, Derek, walked up behind her and smirked. His freckles glowed under the stage lights and his thick red hair had been flattened above the ears, then stuck straight out around the base of his neck. Total cap hair.

"Watch out world, the psychos are coming," he said dryly.

"Omigosh! You are *so* funny!" Donna replied sarcastically, turning to him. "Why don't you take that act on the road? Like, *tonight*. Really. It's time for you to go."

"Shut up, loser," he said, pulling her into a hug. "Congrats."

She hugged him back, closing her eyes and smiling. "You, too."

The Policastro twins may have talked a big game, but deep down they totally loved each other. And me. We had been an inseparable threesome ever since kindergarten when Rhonda Sickle, a horrible, buck-toothed first grader, had stolen my tricycle on the playground and the twins had thrown pinecones at her until she gave it back. Probably the most exhilarating moment of my life. Yeah, we don't get a lot of excitement around Lake Logan, New York. Tons of Canadian geese every spring and fall, but not much excitement.

That was why I was so stoked to be graduating. Don't get me wrong, I love my little town and (almost) all the people in it. I love being able to ride my horse, Lola, wherever I want and not have to worry about getting blindsided by a big rig. I love long evening strolls down by the lake in the summer. I love that almost everyone grows their own tomatoes and corn and that the older ladies in town are constantly bickering over who makes the best raspberry jam. But I knew there was a lot more to life than Lake Logan. And I was kind of dying to find out what was out there. That, and I couldn't wait to be living in a place where not every resident had witnessed my bikini top coming off in the lake at the July Fourth celebration when I was thirteen—a humiliation that was brought up far too often by way too many people. Okay, so UVM wasn't in the middle of a bustling metropolis, but at least it was new. And they had stables, so I would be able to bring Lola. Donna was getting out, too— heading for Rutgers University in New Jersey, while Derek would be sticking close to home at Binghamton.

The graduates around us started to break up, heading out into the seats in search of parents and grandparents, sisters, brothers, and cousins. Flashes popped and somewhere someone squealed with delight.

"Oh, no way Alison Thomas's parents just gave her a car," Derek said.

"You're kidding me."

I looked across the auditorium and sure enough, there was Alison, already having shed her shapeless black gown to expose the mini-dress underneath. She was waving a key of some kind in the air and gripping her father around the neck as her mom took pictures. Alison was the richest kid in our class. The only rich kid, actually. She was also the most . . . *friendly*, if you know what I mean.

"Here comes Dino," Derek said.

"Look away before the saliva starts spraying," Donna deadpanned.

But I couldn't. It was like watching a train wreck. Dino Anderson walked right up to Alison and stuck his tongue down her throat right there in front of her parents. Blech. She squealed with delight as he dipped her backward. Her parents actually laughed. Double blech.

"There is one sight I am *not* going to miss," I said.

Although inside, I actually felt a twinge of sorrow and maybe a smattering of jealousy. Here I was, eighteen years old and a high school graduate, and I had yet to be kissed. I guess that was what happened when you only had sixty boys in your class to choose from and you had endured their awkward phases right along with them. It was kind of hard to get all hot and bothered about someone when you had seen them pee in their pants in third grade like Linus Kaplan, or dig at his chicken pox scabs incessantly all the way through geometry class like Danny Figis. Yeah, the pickins were slim.

"Cassie! Cassie! Over here!"

I smiled when I saw my mom waving at me maniacally while my dad held the ages-old video camera up to his eye. Since I'm an only child, this was pretty much the most exciting event in my parents' lives. I lifted my diploma and waved in return.

"Come down here and let us get a picture of the three of you together!" my mother called.

"You got it, Mrs. Grace," Derek said, loping down the stairs.

As he always did when it came time to pose, Derek got in between me and Donna to keep things symmetrical. My mother squinted at her newish digital camera, holding it a full arm's length away from her face. The woman should have never tried to master new technology. Every picture she took either sliced off someone's head, or took the person on the end completely out of the frame.

The flash went off and we broke apart as Donna and Derek's parents joined us. Donna went to hug her mom and dad and I did the same with mine. As always, my mom's hug was soft but firm and she smelled of lilac perfume with just a hint of the stable scent underneath.

"We're so proud of you, sweetheart," she said, kissing my forehead and tucking my wavy blond hair behind my ear. I looked back into the green eyes that were exactly like my own and smiled. Inside, I actually felt some tears welling up.

"Thanks, Mom."

"And the program says you graduated with honors," my father interrupted, holding the camera down at his side now and holding *up* the little blue-and-white program. "Why didn't you tell us that?"

I shrugged happily. "Thought it would be a nice surprise."

"It sure was. Congratulations, Cass." He pulled me to his side in a half hug and squeezed. As always, I was dwarfed by my six-foot-four-inch father, my head hitting him right where his arm met his side. With his square jaw, stubble, and omnipresent cowboy hat, my dad looked just like the Marlboro man—without the cigarette, of course.

"Come on, everyone! Let's hit the lake!" Michael shouted out, earning a round of whoops and hollers from the graduates dotted around the room. He swung his big, beefy arm in the air and led the charge of the jocks up to the back door.

"I guess we're going," I said, as the room buzzed anew with excitement.

Every year the graduating class camped out on the beach on Lake Logan on graduation night. No underclassmen whatsoever were allowed and everyone brought coolers full of drinks and food, then circulated from tent to tent, sharing everything. There were always rumors of chug lines, drug experimentation, and random hook-ups, but no one knew for sure what went on since none of us had ever been to one. I was pretty much dying to experience it firsthand.

"All right. But don't get home too late," my father said.

"Dad! It's called an all-nighter for a reason," I said teasingly.

He clucked his tongue. "You're the one who wanted to take on more responsibilities this summer," he reminded me. "You've got Shelby Shahanian coming to the ranch at nine A.M. tomorrow for her first lesson."

"I know this, Dad. And I'll be there," I told him. "But this is one Lake Logan ritual that I am not passing up."

He eyed me dubiously, then finally nodded. "All right, but be good."

I rolled my eyes. "I *will* be." Couldn't he see I wasn't a little kid anymore?

"No drinking, no smoking, no . . . anything else," my mom said with a little shudder. Just then, Derek, Donna, and their parents rejoined us for the stroll back up the aisle.

"Come on, Mrs. Grace. It can't be that bad," Donna cajoled. "Sheriff Griffin and Deputy Do-Right check in all the time. They've never shut it down."

"All right," my mom said, giving me another squeeze. "Have fun."

"You'll keep an eye on my little girl, right Derek?" my father said, slapping him on the back so hard he almost took a header into row G.

"You bet, Mr. Grace," he said, coughing as he regained his footing.

I groaned as Donna slung her arm over my shoulder and we followed them up the aisle.

"Hey! It's only a couple more months and then you'll be making your own rules," Donna whispered to me.

My grimace changed to a grin and I hugged her close to my side as we walked. She always knew exactly what to say to cheer me up.

Chapter Two

"So, this is Senior Night," I said, leaning back on my elbows on top of the fleece blanket the twins and I had laid out. I could feel how cold the soft sand was underneath. Even in late June, upstate New York can be pretty damn chilly, especially after the sun goes down. Summer had already started, but most of us were wearing sweatshirts and jeans and a bunch of people were gathered around the mid-sized fire we had started for marshmallow roasting.

"This is Senior Night," Donna confirmed, looking around.

"Kind of lame, no?" I said.

"Hey! It's just getting started!" Derek protested, dropping down at my side with a couple of cans of root beer.

"Are you kidding me with this stuff?" Donna said, tossing the can into the sand. "Where's the goods?"

"I didn't bring any 'goods,'" Derek said sarcastically, making air quotes. "We come home with even a trace of alcohol smell on us and Mom and Dad will kill us first and ask questions later."

"My brother the goody-goody," Donna said, narrowing her eyes.

"My sister the lush," he countered.

She scoffed and got up, dusting off the back of her legs. "I'm gonna go see what Dino and those guys brought. I'll be right back."

She loped off through the sand toward the tent Dino and the other loudmouths from our class had pitched. At least a dozen empty beer cans already littered the area around their cooler, and Dino and Alison were going at it in a flimsy beach chair like there was no tomorrow.

"Those two seriously need to get a room," Derek said, taking a swig of his root beer.

"Or at least a tree," I replied, lifting my chin.

Mara Winters and Lawrence Dodd, couple of the year, were making their way along the sand toward the woods, their arms latched around each other. She laid her head on his shoulder and he kissed the top of it as they matched each other stride for stride. They looked so perfectly in synch moving together, like they were attached at the hip. I knew that if I tried to walk like that with a guy, I'd be so awkward and nervous I'd probably trip us both right into the lake.

"Looks like a lot of people are pairing off," Derek said.

He pointed out another couple headed off in the opposite direction from Mara and Lawrence. From this distance, I couldn't make out who they were. I looked out at the teeny tiny waves lapping at the shore and sighed.

"What's the matter, Cass?" Derek said, nudging my shoulder with his elbow. "Senior night just not wild enough for you?"

"I got something that will help!" Donna sing-songed.

She returned to the blanket with three beers, dropping one in front of each of us. Derek and I both let ours lie, but Donna popped hers open and took a long swig.

"Oh, ick!" she said, sticking out her tongue. "This tastes like ass!"

"And how, exactly, do you know what ass tastes like?" I asked her.

She pulled back and whacked me in the shoulder with the back of her hand. Then she held her breath and took another drink. Donna was nothing if not always ready to party. I had always admired her ability to try new things and let go. Whenever I tried to do it with her, I always ended up talking myself out of it by panicking about the potential consequences.

"So, what's the problem?" Donna asked me. "Irritated that everybody's got a Neanderthal to snuggle except you?"

I laughed. "Well, when you put it that way . . ."

"No! I'm with you," Donna said, taking another sip. "I'd give anything for a little action."

"Okay, *so* didn't need to hear that," Derek said, wincing.

"Donna! You just said they were all Neanderthals!" I reminded her.

"I know! But at this point I would make out with Linus Kaplan if I had to," she said, pointing at the class dork who was actually playing chess across the way with his one friend, Vikram. "I mean, it's Senior Night! We're supposed to get crazy!"

"I don't know," I replied. "I wouldn't mind having someone to sneak off with, but it couldn't be just anyone. It would have to be someone special. Someone I had a real connection with. I don't think I could just kiss someone random."

"See? Now there's a good woman," Derek said, pointing at me with his root beer. "That's what I love about you, Cass. You got a good head on your shoulders. Always count on Cassie to do the right thing."

I blushed. "Okay, could you make me sound any more boring? I'm so sick of being Ms. Reliable."

"So? Do something about it. You should go crazy this summer," Donna suggested, waving her beer can around. "Do something wild."

"Like what?" What the heck was there to do in Lake Logan that was out of the ordinary?

"Kiss Linus Kaplan!" Donna shouted at the top of her lungs.

"Donna!" I hissed.

Linus and Vikram looked up from their chess game and Linus went so pale I thought he was going to pee in his pants again. I felt like I was about to die from embarrassment.

"I think I'm going to go put my feet in the water," I said loudly, pushing myself up. I had to put some distance between me and Linus before he started thinking he had a chance.

"Cass, it's like forty degrees in that lake," Derek said.

"Call it my something wild," I threw over my shoulder.

Of course, Donna and Derek both followed after me. They think *I'm* predictable? I knew there was no way they were going to sit there while I went down to the water. We rarely, if ever, left each other's sides when we were at the same party. Even for a second.

I rolled up my jeans to just below my knee and took off my sneakers and socks. Just the touch of my bare feet against the sand sent serious chills all throughout my body. A little breeze kicked up, adding insult to injury. Still, there was no stopping me now. I took a deep breath of the clean, crisp air and stepped right into the lake.

Holy mother of all that is good in the universe! my brain cried. *What do you think you're doing, you psycho?*

My friends eyed me with amused interest, but I turned away from them and bit my lip against the dry ice sensation that was running its way over my skin. When I turned back to them again, I was pretty sure I looked totally calm.

"It's really not that bad," I said.

"Uh-huh," Derek replied skeptically.

"Cassie, if standing in four inches of freezing water is your 'something wild,' then it's kind of pathetic," Donna said, taking a sip of her beer.

I sighed. "I think I might need to save the rebellion for next year," I told her. "This summer is all about making money for that entry fee so that Lola and I can compete. I need that prize money for school."

I had won a partial scholarship to the University of Vermont, based on my grades and my application essay to the zoological program. Dad was covering the rest of the tuition, but there was nothing to use as spending money. Unless I wanted to work two jobs my entire freshman year, I had to win that novice jumper competition. Twenty thousand dollars would really go a long way in easing the financial pain over the next few years. A *long* way.

"I know," Donna said. "But it's our last summer. Do you really have to work twenty-four seven?"

My heart gave a pang at her words. Our last summer. It was so weird to think of life as anything but this. Me, Donna, and Derek. Lake Logan. Chilling at their family's movie theater or at Pete's Diner or riding horses at our ranch. It really was all coming to an end.

"I'm sure we'll have tons of time to hang out," I said. "I'll make the time."

Donna smiled and I smiled back.

"But for the most part, yeah, I have to work," I told them. "A lot."

"Like I said!" Derek announced, throwing his hands up. "Cassandra Grace. Reliable. Predictable."

I caught Donna's eye and I knew from the wicked smile on her face that she was thinking the exact same thing I was. We pounced on Derek at the exact same moment and he made a move to flee, but he was two seconds too late.

"Predictable this!" I cried.

He let out an intense scream as Donna and I flung him clean into the lake. Both of us were splashed all over, but it was entirely worth it just to see Derek sputter and flail as he resurfaced. His hair was plastered over his eyes and his sweatshirt sleeves pulled down to cover his hands.

"You're dead! You guys are so dead!" he cried, trying to find his footing.

But it was too late. Donna and I had already grabbed my sneakers from the sand and taken off toward the trees, just hoping not to stumble on any half-naked lovers as we ran.

Chapter Three

"That's right, Shelby! Just sit up straight in the saddle and squeeze!" I called out as Shelby and her horse, Patrick (named after SpongeBob's starfish friend), cantered around the paddock. Patrick was a beautiful horse and the Shahanians kept him well. His nut-brown hide shone in the early morning sun and he held up his head and tail as he moved, as if he knew how pretty he was. Shelby smiled as she took the turns, brown braids flying. At age nine, she was a natural. This was only the first day of her second summer of lessons and I could already tell that by the end of August, she would be ready to compete in her age group.

Early last summer, my father had been surprised when Shelby and her mother had shown up at our front door in the middle of dinner, asking about riding lessons. Most people knew that our house and our stable, while on the same property, were two separate entities. One was for business, the other for family. Our ranch-style house sat atop a small hill, the west-facing windows looking out over the stable, the paddock, and the fields down below. Our driveway ran between the paddock and the grazing field, then cut left and rounded a clump of trees as it climbed the slope. It finally cut back right and ended in the dirt lot just outside our porch door. Vendors, trainers, vets, and riding students almost never drove past the stable and came to our front door—especially not after business hours.

Dad had been ready to toss the Shahanians out, but when I heard them mention me, I had immediately joined them at the door. It turned out they had asked around and someone had recommended I teach little Shelby. I never found out where they had gotten my name, but I had been begging my dad to let me take on my own clients for two years. And there was someone specifically asking for me. How could he turn that down?

Well, he couldn't. It turned out that Mrs. Shahanian's offer of $100 an hour, coupled with my big, begging doe eyes, nudged Dad into agreeing. Last year I ended up having three other students aside from Shelby, and this year I had landed even more.

I glanced at my watch as Shelby and Patrick came around the last turn. Her hour was almost up. Easiest hundred bucks I would ever make. Unfortunately, fifty percent went directly to the ranch—which was the same for the other instructor; an old family friend named Penny Haberman. Another forty my parents made me put into my untouchable savings account, which I couldn't go near until I graduated college—a little agreement I had made with my parents when I had first started teaching. That meant that I had just made a whopping ten bucks to either use as spending money or put toward the competition entrance fee. It was going to take me a lot of lessons to earn that money before the competition on the third weekend of August—especially if I wanted to have any kind of a life this summer. I mean, it would be nice to be able to buy myself the occasional ice cream cone.

"Okay, Shelby! Bring him in!" I called out.

"'Kay!"

Down at the bottom of the drive, Mrs. Shahanian's black Mercedes SUV signaled and turned in. I smiled and tried not to shake my head. All the summer locals drove high-end cars, but not all of them were as nice as Mrs. Shahanian's.

Shelby and her family were not year-round Lake Logan natives. They were what we actual townspeople called "summer locals" or, more commonly and less charitably, "invaders." Dotted all around the periphery of our lovely hamlet—many of them on or near the remote shore of the lake—were huge Victorian mansions, all of which were deserted nine to ten months out of the year. They were vacation homes for the wealthy—those who considered themselves too old-school or too humble to hit the Hamptons with the rest of New York City's elite. Instead they wended their way north every June or July in their Lexus convertibles, their Jaguars, their BMWs, and took over the town of Lake Logan. They bought up our fresh corn, lamented about our lack of espresso bars, and looked down their noses at us whenever they got the chance. The Lake Logan Country Club became a swinging site for balls and charity events and the omnipresent "Summer Fling," an event to which all their teen sons and daughters flocked in their designer gowns and tuxes. Inevitably there would be a drunken caravan of limos and sports cars through the center of town, these overprivileged kids waving their champagne bottles out the windows—laughing and showing off. They were all such prize losers.

Not that I'm bitter or anything.

"How did I do?" Shelby asked, dismounting with ease and dropping to the ground.

I sighed and smiled. Cute little Shelby. In just a few short years she would be "woo-wooing" her way down Main Street in a strapless Calvin Klein, irritating the crap out of all of us. It was, unfortunately, her destiny. But for now, she was still a sweet, rosy-cheeked kid. And a damn fine rider.

"You did great," I told her, squeezing her chin quickly between my thumb and forefinger.

"I can tell you two have been practicing a lot this year."

"I was at the stables twice a week, every week," Shelby said proudly. "Patrick didn't like being left alone there so I visited him as much as I could."

"You are a very good horse owner," I told her. "And a good friend to Patrick, too."

The Mercedes pulled up a few feet away on the dirt lot and Mrs. Shahanian got out. She was wearing capri pants, high heels, and a tiny tank top. Did I mention that she didn't exactly know how to dress for the country? She was nice, but not all that bright. But at least she was wearing a straw cowboy hat. That would protect her skin from the sun—sort of.

"Hello, Cassie!" she called, waving her hand and smiling as she tottered over in her stilts. "Hey, Shell. How was your first lesson?"

"Cassie thinks I can compete this year," Shelby said with a gap-toothed grin.

"Really? That's great!" her mother replied. "You should have seen her this winter, Cassie. All she can talk about is horses. Her father and I love to see her so excited about something other than television. For a while there when she was younger, we thought she was actually going to morph into Dora the Explorer," she added with a laugh.

"Mo-om!" Shelby protested.

"Well, she's amazing at it," I told Mrs. Shahanian, tucking my hair behind my ears. "I think she was born to be on a horse."

"I have no idea where she gets it," her mother said. She reached out and ran a hand over Shelby's hair. "But we have you to thank for her inspiration."

"Inspiration?" I asked. It was an odd choice of words.

"Last summer I saw you riding Lola over by the lake and I just thought it was the coolest," Shelby said, squinting against the sun as she looked up at me. "That's when I begged my mom for lessons."

"After about an hour of her nonstop pleading, her father and I finally asked around town and found out that you were the mysterious girl on the horse. That was how we ended up here," Mrs. Shahanian explained. "I thought you knew all this."

"No. Never heard the whole story," I said, touched. I couldn't believe that Shelby was riding because she wanted to be like me. As far as I knew, in my entire life, no one else had ever wanted to be like me. Even *I* sometimes wanted to be less like me. Especially in the risk-taking department.

"And it turned out you were the best!" Mrs. Shahanian said. "Speaking of which, I told all my friends about you. Marni Locke should be calling here tomorrow. She wants to bring in her two boys for lessons. And I wouldn't be surprised if there were many more where they came from."

I smiled, dollar signs lighting up in my mind. One good thing about the invaders: They were definitely going to help me inch closer to my monetary goals. Sure, the more lessons I gave, the less time I would have for fun, but let's be honest—there wasn't all that much to do around Lake Logan, anyway.

"We didn't have to go shopping, Dad. I could have had cereal," I said, glancing over my shoulder at my father as we walked out of Wonder

Mart, our local food market.

"*You* could have had cereal," he said, pulling a green pepper out of the brown paper bag he was holding. He tossed it up and caught it. "But when a man needs a Spanish omelet, he needs a Spanish omelet."

I laughed as my stomach rumbled. I had inhaled a banana and some juice before Shelby's lesson, but by the time she was done, I was starving. We were putting Patrick up for the summer while the Shahanians had a stable built on their property—a $200,000 project, from what I understood—a lot to spend on a nine-year-old's hobby, no matter how good she was at it. But I digress. Keeping Patrick meant that I had to brush him, rub him down, and feed him. The Shahanians paid extra to rent the stall for all the extra work, but it was a lot to take care of, as well as all of our horses, and Penny had the day off. When I emerged from the stable after taking care of all the horses, Dad was on his way out on his omelet quest. Trudging to the pickup had seemed easier than the hike back up to the house, so I had offered to come along.

Dad opened the door of our rusty old truck,

which squealed horribly, and placed the grocery bag on the vinyl seat. I plopped down, avoiding the faulty spring under the passenger's side. My mother, who usually had to drive twenty miles to the grade school to teach every day, had the newer car. Dad always maintained that as long as the truck was running, it was good enough to get him where he needed to go. My mom thought it was an eyesore, but I liked the old thing. It was rugged and reliable, just like my dad.

I rolled down the window, then leaned forward and flicked on the radio. Music blasted so loud I jumped and fumbled for the knob. It was a good two seconds before I realized the wailing guitar was not coming from our crappy old speakers.

"Here comes the caravan," my father said.

I looked past the open driver's side door where my dad stood and saw the gleaming silver Lexus sedan gliding by. Behind it was a red sports car—a model I had never seen before and the source of the rock concert—with a guy younger than me behind the wheel, head-banging along. A couple seconds after they passed, a Hummer and a BMW convertible followed. I

saw a teenage girl in the backseat of the convertible, gabbing away on a cell phone while
she checked her manicured nails.

"They're heee-*ere*!" I sing-songed.

My dad laughed and shook his head,
scratching at a couple days' growth on his chin.
He dropped into the seat and slammed the door
of the truck.

"Sometimes I wonder why we tolerate them
taking over our town every summer," my father
said.

"Because they rent stalls and hire us for lessons and after one more summer it's all going to
pay for the brand new stables?" I suggested
innocently.

My dad grinned. "Oh yeah. That's why," he
said with a wink. He turned the key and revved
the loud engine. "Let's go make us some breakfast."

After a long day of chores and exercising Lola,
I borrowed Dad's truck and headed into town
to hang with Donna and Derek at the theater.
The Regency Theater was an old movie house
built back in the 1950s by Donna and Derek's

grandfather, who had the idea of bringing a little Hollywood glamour to Lake Logan. From the pictures that hung in Mr. Policastro's tiny office, the place was once a glittering beacon in the center of an otherwise sleepy town. But in my lifetime the multi-hundred-lightbulb REGENCY sign had never once been lit, and the burgundy-and-gold carpets just kept wearing thinner and thinner. The Regency only had one screen and a balcony that had long since been roped off by some state official due to the building's lack of "structural integrity." Scary as that phrase was, it didn't stop me from hanging out there almost every weekend night during the year and every single night during the summer.

Where else did we have to go?

That night, Donna and I hung out behind the concessions counter and emptied the cabinet of every last one of the gummy bears boxes. Our plan was to make a huge candy box castle on the counter to pass the time. Derek sat on the back counter next to the popper—a big no-no by his father's standards—and read an old Stephen King novel. Both he and Donna were sporting the Regency uniform: black pants, white shirt, black bowtie, hideous maroon suit jacket.

"Are your parents going to get any *good* movies this summer?" I asked as I built the base of our colorful castle.

"Just the usual lineup of cartoons and badly written inspirational flicks starring awful child actors," Derek said with a sigh.

"In other words, nothing that any of us would remotely want to see," I replied.

As we spoke, the latest Disney 'toon was playing in the theater. The only people in there as far as I knew were the Marlin family—Dad, Mom, Melissa and Marissa—who showed up every Saturday night like clockwork, and Alison and Dino, who sometimes could find no better place to make out than the back of the theater.

"Dad is never going to make any money off of this place if he doesn't start getting some better stuff," Donna said, propping her head on her hand. She stared across the lobby at the framed poster advertising next week's film—something about a boy and his baseball. "Like something with explosions and curse words and sex."

"Or at least just one of the three," I put in,

balancing one box on top of another.

"Never gonna happen," Derek said. He pushed himself off the counter and came over to help me. "Dad is nothing if not a purist. Grandpa built this theater to be a family place and Dad is never going to change that."

"This is going to be the most boring summer ever!" Donna lamented, collapsing fully on top of the candy case. Her arms splayed out across the glass as she pressed her cheek into it. "Hey!" she said, lifting her head minutely. "Do you think the Kents will show this year?"

Derek and I exchanged a "here we go" glance and rolled our eyes. "Donna—"

"What? It could happen! They could be on their way here right now in their gold-plated stretch limos," she said, growing animated.

"Now, now, Donna. I'm sure that if the Kents have limos, they're *solid* gold, not gold *plated*," Derek said, kneading his sister's shoulders.

"My mistake," Donna said sarcastically. "But seriously, their housekeepers and maintenance guys were up there last week and Courtney Billup said they even cleaned up the tennis court with leaf blowers. They *never* clean off the tennis court."

"How would Courtney Billup know?" I asked. "No one can even see into the Kents' backyard."

I could, though. And had, many, many times. In fact, I already knew about the tennis courts. I also knew that the pool had been filled with new water and the garage had been completely cleaned out. All this thanks to my daily, and illegal, morning rides with Lola. No one, not even Donna and Derek, knew that I rode her through the Kents' property every morning. My one transgression in life. But it was a sin just to leave all that lush property sitting there unenjoyed.

"Her brother Andrew was on the crew," Donna said, crossing her arms over her chest. "What do you think about that?"

"Not much," I replied with a sigh. "We go through this same conversation every year, and every year the Kents don't come, no matter what their staff does to prepare their house. I don't see what the big deal is, anyway. They're just another family of invaders."

"Cassie, please," Donna said. "Even you have to be a *little* curious."

"Nope. Not one bit," I said, placing the final box on top of my castle.

But I was. A little. Everyone in town was. The Kent family was at the heart of every gossipy conversation I had ever heard. Their house was the most gorgeous manse in the entire town, sitting atop Hull Hill, which overlooked the lake. It had at least eight gables, two turrets, an immense wraparound porch, and a detached garage that could house four cars. The swimming pool was Olympic-sized and had a swirly slide. The tennis court had been dug up and reset with red clay a couple of years ago, even though not a soul had played on it since. Their property stretched for a hundred acres and included woods, a fishing stream, and at least twenty acres of open field. It was, in truth, a perfect vacation spot—if you weren't from around here. One that hadn't been used since before I was born. Except by me and Lola.

No one in my generation had ever laid eyes on a Kent. Each year they sent an entire staff of cleaners, landscapers, plumbers, and carpenters to survey the house and do any work that needed to be done. For a week the place would be a flurry of action—saws buzzing, dust flying, bags of leaves being toted away. Then the staff would move out, leaving everything spotless, and the whole town would hold their breath. Would this be the summer that the Kents finally decided to grace us with their presence? Would we at last get to see the woman who young Susan Morris had grown up to be?

Twenty years ago Susan Morris had been a local girl and recent graduate like myself when, by all reports, the young and devastatingly handsome Robert Kent had come into town with his grandparents and swept her off her feet. They had married in secret and Susan had gone off with Robert to live in Manhattan, never communicating with her family again. From everything the old biddies in town had told us over the years, both of Susan's parents had eventually died of broken hearts. I thought that was a little extreme—a little drama made up by our aging town gossips for their own entertainment—but hey, you never know.

"Do you think Robert Kent really looks

exactly like James Bond?" Donna asked, staring off wistfully into space.

"Which one?" Derek joked.

"If it's Pierce Brosnan, good. If it's Sean Connery, *bad*," I put in.

Derek laughed but Donna didn't even seem to hear me.

"I heard they have this huge mansion in the Hamptons right down the beach from Ralph Lauren," Donna said. "If I had a place like that, I'd never come up here either. I mean, why hang out with us when you can hang out with P. Diddy and the Hilton sisters?"

"Please. We are way cooler than those ho's," I replied with a laugh.

"I hear that," Donna said, lifting her hand for a high five. She sighed and listlessly knocked over my carefully built gummy tower.

"Hey!" I protested as boxes tumbled over the counter and onto the floor.

"It's not like we don't have time to build another one," she said.

Derek walked around the counter and started cleaning up after his sister — a sight that was all too common. As he piled the boxes back up in front of me, Donna didn't even offer to help. She was the messer, he was the cleaner.

"Maybe they'll come this year," she said, scooping out a mini cup of popcorn for herself, then two more for me and Derek. "Maybe they'll instinctively sense that an entire town is about to perish out of sheer inactivity and they'll swoop in to save us all."

Derek laughed and I patted Donna on the back. "If they do, I'm sure you'll be disappointed," I told her, snagging a piece of popcorn and dropping it into my mouth. "There is absolutely no way that these people are half as interesting as everyone hopes they'll be."

Chapter Four

Behind our ranch, the hill continued up for about a quarter of a mile of tree-covered property, then flattened out for half a mile and started the descent on the other side. I had been exploring the woods back there with my parents ever since I was a little girl. Back when I was in grade school, they hardly ever let me go alone, concerned I might stumble across a black bear or get lost on one of the many winding paths. But as I got older, I started taking Lola out for longer and longer rides, discovering corners of the property that I had never seen. Together Lola and I had found an old cave peppered with graffiti dating back to the 1920s—some carved into the rock, some spray-painted—and a broken-down shack that had been there for no one knew how long.

We had also discovered a shortcut to the lush and unused property surrounding the Kent estate. Who knew the lowly local Graces lived so close to greatness? I had only realized it because of all the "No Trespassing" signs tacked to trees and attached to spikes that were driven into the ground. For people who were never around, the Kents were certainly paranoid. Unfortunately for them, the warnings didn't work on me. In fact, they kind of spurred me along. Who did these people think they were, forbidding anyone to step foot on the property that they barely even knew was there? As far as I was concerned, someone should be able to appreciate the beauty of that estate. And that someone was going to be me.

The day after our gummy bears castle night, I got up extra early and took Lola out for our regular ride. We walked up the winding pathway, past the old oak that had been felled by a lightning strike two years before, and then out onto the meadow at the top of the hill, where the Kent property began. As always, I ignored the large orange-and-black sign bolted to the oak at the end of the path and loosened up on the reins. Lola was so used to this routine that she knew it was coming, and sped up a bit before I even nudged her with my heels. I sat forward in the saddle as we raced along, enjoying the cool morning air as it whipped my hair back.

At the far end of the meadow, the trees rose up again and I slowed Lola as we approached. She instantly dropped to a canter and I urged her to the left. I planned to ride along the tree line in the shade, then take her through the woods and down toward the Kent house. When it came down to it, I was more curious about the improvements the staff had made to the empty mansion than I was about the Kent family. It seemed insane to me that these people spent all that money every year to keep the house up and never set foot in it. What kind of people had cash to burn like that?

Lola and I were about to turn down our regular path when I heard the sudden roar of an engine — it sounded like a chainsaw starting up or a boat revving to life. Lola whinnied and I whipped my head around, looking for the source of the noise. Suddenly a blur of red and black shot right out of the woods in front of us, into the meadow.

Clouds of dust kicked up, temporarily blinding me as Lola reared back and raised her front hoofs. I coughed and blinked my stinging eyes, gripping her reins with one hand while patting her neck with the other. It was an automatic reaction, trying to calm her down even though *my* heart was pounding from the shock. If Lola got spooked and took off, it wouldn't be good for either one of us.

Finally I felt all of Lola's feet hit the ground. She steadied and I was able to wipe my hand across my eyes. Through the watery blur, I saw a bobbing, helmeted head atop an ATV, circling around the center of the meadow and heading back in our direction. I leaned down on Lola's neck and patted her, whispering soothing tones into her ear. The ATV skidded to a stop a few feet away.

"What are you doing, you psycho?" I shouted. "You almost killed us!"

Normally, I'm not the yelling kind, but my adrenaline was up and my pulse was pounding in my ears. Two seconds later and Lola and I would have been maimed.

The driver ripped his helmet off and my breath caught in my throat. As angry as I was, I knew that I had never seen anyone this beautiful before in my life—at least not outside of *InStyle* magazine. The driver was about my age with sharp blue eyes and brown hair, most of which was plastered to his forehead with sweat. He had a square jaw and a tiny bit of scruff on his chin and cheekbones. Usually I would have been intimidated by the way he was glaring at me, but anger was a good look for him. He wore blue jeans, a light blue T-shirt, and a black-and-red leather racing jacket that looked as if it had been through a hurricane.

"Me!?" he shouted, standing up and tossing his helmet aside. He swung his leg over his ATV and stormed over to us. "You shouldn't even be here! You're trespassing on my property."

I laughed automatically, but then my heart sank and my throat went dry. "Your property?" I asked. "You're not—"

"Jared Kent," he said, pulling his riding gloves off.

Jared Kent. An actual Kent. The Kents were actually *here*. Donna was going to flip out when she heard about—

"And yeah, this heap of dirt is my property," he added.

Ugh! My awe and excitement was cut short just like that. Clearly the Kents were actually as obnoxious as I had always imagined. Gorgeous, I'll admit—at least this guy was— but obnoxious.

"Heap of dirt?" I replied, regaining my composure. "This is the most beautiful piece of land in upstate New York!"

"Oooh! Trees and grass! I'm so impressed," Jared said, waggling his fingers. "I can get that in Central Park, thanks."

"I knew it," I said with a laugh. "I knew you people didn't deserve to have this place."

"Excuse me?" he replied, raising his eyebrows.

"You heard me. This plot has been sitting here ignored for years and then you come out of nowhere and accuse *me* of trespassing!" I said, surprised at myself. Apparently adrenaline brought out the sarcasm in me.

"Well you are, aren't you?" he shot back.

"At least I appreciate this place!" I replied, patting Lola as she stepped sideways a bit. She wasn't much for yelling.

"Well it *belongs* to me," Jared replied. "So I think my rights trump yours."

"Typical," I said sarcastically. "It's all about who owns what. It's not like Lola and I are hurting anything riding through here. You and your ATV, however, probably just ripped up tons of grass and scared away a couple dozen animals with your little joyride." He snorted a laugh, but didn't have a comeback. I was kind of on a high-and-mighty roll.

"Who the heck *are* you, anyway?" he asked.

"Who the heck are you?" I shot back without thinking.

"I already told you that," he said.

I flushed. "Oh . . . right." So much for my roll.

Jared glanced at me, then cracked up laughing. My heart pitter-pattered in my chest, and suddenly I found myself grinning uncontrollably. Our indignation had started to sound kind of absurd—to both of us, apparently. And if anger was a good look for him, laughter was ten times better.

He's a Kent, Cassie, I told myself. *An* invader. *Get a grip.*

I sighed and dismounted, dropping to the ground in front of him. He had a couple of inches on me and had the best posture I had ever seen on a guy, holding his shoulders back and his chin up. There was a small brown birthmark next to his left eye. Totally cute. I cleared my throat and looked at the ground. If I didn't watch out, I was going to be in huge trouble here. We all knew what happened the last time a local girl found a Kent boy attractive. She became the central character of gossip for the next twenty years.

"I'm Cassandra Grace. This is Lola," I said finally.

"Lola. A pleasure," he said with a quick nod at my horse. She snorted and he grinned.

"May as well tell you now that I ride through here every morning," I admitted. "You can call the police, but they're both good friends of the family, so I'm not sure you'll get anywhere."

"*Both* of them?" Jared said, pulling his chin back. "Big precinct you got up here."

· 46 ·

"It's just a room at town hall, but it gets the job done," I said, aware that he was teasing the town already, but chose to ignore it. It was, after all, typical invader behavior. Besides, what did I care what he thought? After this conversation I was sure I would never speak to him again. Invaders didn't talk to locals unless they were buying corn from them or paying for an oil change. Not that any of us were interested in forging deeper relationships with people who paid more money for their shoes than we did for our cars.

Jared laughed and kicked at the dirt. "You have no idea how cool it is to meet you, Cassandra Grace."

"Cassie," I said. My heart had skipped a beat when he said my name. Damn it. "And why?"

"I thought this town was going to be full of old fogies and bores," he said. "But you are clearly neither of those."

"We have lots of people who don't fall into either of those categories," I shot back. "Tons."

Jared shoved his driving gloves into the back pocket of his jeans. "Care to prove it?" he challenged.

I glanced at my watch and smirked. Okay, so maybe this conversation was going to go a little further. But only because I wanted to wipe that superior smirk off his face.

"Love to," I said.

Considering I had rolled out of bed that morning, braided my hair, mucked out the stalls, fed the horses, and gone directly on my ride, I was fairly noxious at this point and in desperate need of a shower. I told Jared to give me forty-five minutes and gave him directions to the ranch.

"Just don't pick me up on that thing," I said, pointing at the ATV.

"Don't worry. I just got a new car and I've been dying to take it out again," he replied.

Shocker.

Mom was at work—the elementary school got out two weeks after the high school did—and Dad was at my Uncle Rod's helping him patch a hole in his garage roof. (Uncle Rod's not really my uncle, but growing up in a small community, we all ended up calling our parents' friends "uncle" this or "aunt" that.) I pinned my hair up and showered quickly, then undid my braids and let my hair fall down over my shoulders in waves. Then I threw on my favorite jeans and sneakers and changed my shirt four times, then ripped off the last one, feeling ashamed of myself. I was not going to dress up for an invader. Not this girl.

Finally I pulled on my A&W Root Beer T-shirt—a favorite of mine for its kitsch value that unfortunately did nothing for my complexion—and walked out to wait for Jared.

He was ten minutes late and the music blared from his car stereo speakers as he sped up the dirt drive. I had to wave my hand in front of my face to clear the dust as he paused in front of me. His new car was a two-door BMW sports thing in gunmetal silver with black leather seats. The top was, of course, down.

"Hop in," he said with a grin.

His hair was clean now and was all tousled, but looked perfect anyway. My pulse responded to the sight of him by rushing annoyingly through my ears. No one had ever had this kind of effect on me before. I had to get a grip.

I opened the door and sunk into the creamy leather seat in what I hoped was a casual way.

It was the cleanest car I had ever seen.

"So, where to?" he asked.

"Know how to get downtown?" I asked, laying my arm on top of the door.

"Downtown. That's funny," he said. "You sure one gas station and a library qualifies?"

"You are hysterical," I said flatly.

He revved the engine a few times, showing off, then peeled out. I gripped the door and seat as he flew down the driveway and zoomed onto Town Line Road without so much as a glance over his shoulder.

"Don't worry! I'm a great driver!" he shouted over the roar of the air whipping by.

I fumbled for my seat belt and locked it in as we flew past trees and fences in a blur.

"You might want to slow down. People have animals around here and, you know, children," I told him.

"Live a little!" Jared shouted, downshifting and taking the turn onto Main Street. The tires squealed, and when I looked behind us, we had left track marks on the asphalt. Soon Mr. Crawley's vegetable stand at the edge of town loomed into view, then blurred by.

"We're almost there!" I said, hoping *that* might slow him down. "It's Pete's Diner up here on the right!"

Jared slammed on the brakes and I shot forward, the seat belt cutting into my skin. He cut the wheel and whirled into a parking space right at the end of the small parking lot. It took a full five seconds before I could breathe again.

"Sweet ride, right?" he said, climbing out over the car door.

"Yeah," I said, hoping I hadn't peed in my pants. "Sweet."

Jared walked around and opened my door for me. I looked up, surprised at the gentlemanly gesture. I wasn't surprised, however, when my knees quaked under me. Jared noticed my unsteadiness and laughed.

"You know, Gracie, if we're going to hang out, you're going to have to loosen up," he said, patting me on the back.

"It's Cassie. Cassandra *Grace*," I replied. "And who says we're going to hang out?"

"We are. You like me already. I can tell," he said, slamming the door. "And I think I'll call you Gracie," he said with a half smile, now opening the screen door to Pete's.

I rolled my eyes, but couldn't help smiling at his cocky grin. The kid was charming. The only problem was, he knew it.

The second we stepped through the door at Pete's, I knew I had made a mistake. Mr. Lutz and Mr. Smith—both retired farmers with more wrinkles than a saddlebag—were hunched at the counter, sipping their coffee. The two oldest fogies in the book. They, along with the ten other people in the place, all turned around and stared at us as I led Jared over to my usual booth. Elaine Mission, Pete's wife and head waitress, nearly dropped the carafe of decaffeinated coffee. I knew they weren't surprised to see me. After all, Donna, Derek, and I met here every other morning for breakfast. What they were surprised about was seeing me, Cassie Grace, with an invader.

From the looks on their faces it was clear what they were thinking. I had gone over to the dark side.

"I think I'm gonna hit the bathroom," Jared said, either not noticing, or choosing not to acknowledge, the stares. "Order me a coffee? Black."

"Sure," I replied.

I slid onto the vinyl seat of the booth and pulled out one of the cardboard-backed menus, even though I had it pretty much memorized. Still, the usual diner noise hadn't started up again. What was with these people? Hadn't they ever seen an invader before?

"Coffee?" Elaine asked, materializing at the end of the table.

She wore a standard blue uniform—a knee-length dress with a white pinafore over it. No nametag, since we all knew who she was. Her curly brown hair was up in a messy bun and, as always, she wore no makeup whatsoever. I had always thought she was a pretty woman for her age, which was pushing sixty. Of all the gabby women in town, she was the gabbiest—always looking for new dirt to share with the patrons of Pete's.

"Thanks, Elaine," I said, trying not to make eye contact. Maybe if I didn't look at her, she wouldn't grill me.

"And for the boy you're with?" she asked.

"Yes. For him, too," I replied.

She turned over two of the four coffee cups on the table and filled them with steaming hot liquid.

"And who *is* the boy you're with?" she asked.

Luckily, I was saved by my hyperventilating best friend. At that exact moment, Donna flung herself through the door, red and out of breath, and clung to the back of the seat across from mine.

"You are *so* not gonna believe this!" she blurted. "The Kents are here!"

Elaine gasped and looked at Maria Roselle, who occupied her usual space at the end of the counter. Maria looked as if she was going to fall off her stool. Everyone in the place was riveted on Donna.

"They came in late last night! They're actually staying for the entire summer! Deputy Do-Right told my dad this morning when he was at the bank! Can you believe it?"

"Actually, I —"

"Omigod, I can't believe they actually *deigned* to come here," Donna said, falling onto the bench. "How are they going to live without their spas and manicurists and chauffeurs?"

"Well, I'm sure they're not *that* bad," I said, glancing over my shoulder toward the rest rooms.

"Please! You *know* they're going to be the first ones to complain about our lack of Starbucks!" Donna said, unable to take a hint in her current state of manic. "But man, I can't wait to see what Susan Kent is like. I can't believe she actually came back here when all anyone's been talking about in this town for twenty years is what a heartless, money-grubbing slut she turned out to be."

Donna's eyes trailed up and over my shoulder and from the look of shock on her face, I knew she had just seen the hot stranger in the room. Unfortunately, she didn't know she had just been bad-mouthing the hot stranger's mom. My stomach tightened into a ball and I looked over my shoulder again. Sure enough, Jared was standing there with his jaw clenched, his fingers curled into fists at his sides. I had only known him for about five seconds, but even I could see the blatant hurt in his eyes.

"Um . . . Jared, this is my best friend, Donna," I said, hoping there was some way to salvage the situation. "Donna, this is Jared," I said, looking her in the eye. "Jared *Kent*."

Donna went as white as Elaine's apron. Luke, the fry cook behind the counter, burst out laughing. I glared at him and waited as everyone else in the room salivated to see what would happen next.

"Well. Looks like I was right about this town after all," Jared said finally.

"Omigod. I'm *so* sorry," Donna began, getting up.

But Jared just stormed right past her and slammed open the door with the heel of his hand. I jumped up and took off after him, running through the door just as Derek came up the steps.

"Cassie? What—"

"Jared! Wait!" I called out. "She didn't mean it!"

But Jared jumped back in his car and sped away—if possible even faster than he had arrived.

Well. So much for that, I thought, feeling an

unexpected twinge of major regret. Not that I expected anything to *happen* between me and Jared. Or wanted it to. I had a lot to do this summer. I didn't need a Kent-sized distraction. But still, it kind of sucked standing there, knowing Donna had hurt his feelings. Knowing that he probably hated me now.

"What the hell was that?" Derek asked, watching with me as the dust and leaves settled on the road.

"That was a Kent," I said, turning and walking back into the diner.

"You're kidding me. That tool?" Derek said.

Donna was still on her feet as the rest of the diner's clientele buzzed over what they had just witnessed. She looked like she was about to throw up.

"Oh, God. What just happened? Did I really just say that right in front of him?" she asked, sitting down and covering her face with her hands.

"What?" Derek asked. "What did you say?"

"She basically just insulted his mother right to his face," I clarified, sitting next to Donna and putting my arm around her.

"Oh, man," Derek said, taking the bench across from us.

"I didn't know! How was I supposed to know he was here?" Donna wailed, dropping her hands. "You!" she said, whirling on me. "You brought him here! How could you bring him here?!"

"What?" I said. "He just told me he wanted to meet some cool people. Obviously I thought of you guys."

Donna gaped at me, then at Derek. "And I called his mother a slut. Yeah. Real cool."

"Come on, Cassie," Derek said, dumping some sugar into what was formerly my coffee. "You really think Jared Kent is interested in being friends with us?"

I blinked and picked up the fork in front of me, toying with it. "Why not? He seemed pretty cool. Egotistical, maybe, but cool. And he's here for the whole summer. Maybe he wants to make new friends."

Derek scoffed. "Yeah, right. He probably just needed someone to slum with until his country club buddies show up."

"You don't know that," I said, though I felt

the sting of truth in my chest. We had never known any invaders who actually hung out with locals. Not as friends, anyway. There were always a few jerks who did everything they could to fool around with a local girl or two, then dump her. It was like their thing. How had I, in ten minutes with Jared, managed to forget that?

"You should probably steer clear of him, Cass," Derek said, taking a sip of his coffee. "He seemed like a class A asshole."

"You only saw him for a second," I pointed out.

"Yeah, but he didn't let either one of us explain or apologize," Donna reminded me.

"And then he peeled outta here like a maniac," Derek said. "He could've killed somebody."

"Well, actually, that was kind of cool," Donna said with a weak smile. "Did you *see* that car? Damn!"

"Tongue back in mouth, sis," Derek joked. "But seriously. If Jared Kent really wants to make new friends, let him find somebody else. You don't need that kind of jerk hanging around."

Good old Derek. So overprotective. We

spent so much time together that half my graduating class always assumed we were a couple, but in reality we were way more like brother and sister. *Big* brother and *little* sister, to be more specific.

"You sound like my dad," I said, my shoulders slumping.

"Hey. I like your dad," Derek said with a smile.

I chuckled and took a sip of Jared's black coffee. As much as my overexcited heart hated to admit it, maybe Derek and Donna were right. I had too much going on this summer to waste time worrying about a hot-headed daredevil who would only be here for two months anyway.

Now all I had to do was erase the memory of those piercing blue eyes from my mind and I would be fine.

Easier said than done.

Chapter Five

"You're kidding. The Kents are actually here?"

My mom turned off the water faucet and dropped her yellow-gloved hands into the soap suds. I had just told her all about my encounter with Jared, and she now looked at me as if I had just announced "Extreme Makeover" was coming in and bulldozing our ranch. Her skin took on this waxy sheen that made me think of my last stomach flu. How had I forgotten that Mom and Mrs. Kent, a.k.a. Susan Morris, a.k.a. Jared's mother, had once been best friends?

"Yeah. Sorry," I said, cringing as I dried the casserole dish. "I guess I should have started that story with some kind of warning. Are you freaked?"

"I guess. A little," Mom said, blowing her

blond bangs off her face. "I mean, I haven't seen Susan in . . . what? Twenty years?" She widened her eyes in disbelief and started scrubbing her sauce pot rather vigorously.

I couldn't even imagine what it would be like not to see Donna for twenty years. I shuddered at the thought of not being able to call her up every night and tell her all about my day. It must have been devastating to lose a best friend so abruptly.

"I shouldn't have brought it up," I said. I felt bad for putting that crease in my mom's forehead. Clearly there were some unresolved issues here and the pot was feeling the brunt of the frustration.

"No. It's all right. I want you to be able to tell me what's going on in your life," she said with a quick glance. "Don't start keeping secrets on my account. The last thing I need is you running around town with this Kent kid and feeling like you can't talk to me about things."

I scoffed and felt a rush of heat rise up my neck. "Believe me, I am not going to be running around town with this Kent kid," I said, grabbing a glass to dry.

"Why?" my mom said. She rinsed the pot, then turned her full attention to me. "What was he like?"

"Obnoxious."

Gorgeous.

"Arrogant."

Smart.

"Reckless."

Exhilarating.

My mother smirked. "Sounds like a Kent."

"But he has to have some good points, too, right?" I said, tilting my head and trying not to look *too* interested. "You were best friends with his mom, so we know she must've been *way* cool."

"Ha ha," my mother said, recognizing my sarcastic jab.

"No, I'm serious," I said. "What was Susan like?"

My mother rinsed another dish and looked through the window at the waning sunlight. She took a deep breath and sighed wistfully. I had seen enough yearbooks and old photos of my mom to know that she was quite the hottie in her day. It was in moments like these that you could totally see the gorgeous girl she had been back then. Not that she wasn't still beautiful, she was just mom-beautiful instead of movie-star-beautiful.

"Susan was funny. She was adventurous and a little wild," she said. Then she looked at me, considering. "Kind of like Donna."

"Ah," I said with a grin. "So I'm boring like you and Donna's wild and cool like Susan."

"I never said either one of us was boring," my mother pointed out. "But Donna does remind me a little bit of her. She had that huge heart that both you girls have. She was *crazy* about animals. Even more so than me. I think she was the only vegetarian ever to grow up in this town."

"Really?" I said, raising my eyebrows.

"Yep. And you should have seen her house. She fed every stray cat and dog that came along," my mother said with a laugh. "It got to the point where her father had to keep a chalkboard with all the animals' names on it so they would be able to count them up and recognize if one went missing. If an animal was still unaccounted for after a couple of days, he would run around the barn and the garage and the basement, checking to see if there was a cat about to give birth."

"Wow. Must've been a lot of hair around," I said.

"She was always covered in it," my mother told me. "You couldn't go over there in your good clothes."

I laughed with her and took the pot out of the rack to dry with the cloth. "It's weird," I said.

"What?"

"I can't imagine a girl like that falling for some player like Mr. Kent is supposed to be. She sounds too independent," I said with a shrug. "How did it happen? What's the real story?"

As many times as I had heard everyone else in town tell the tale, I had never heard my mom talk about it once. She should have been the most reliable source, right? Being that she and Susan were so close.

But the second I asked the question, my mom's face seemed to shut down. She went back to washing the dishes with a new and bizarre level of interest.

"That's all in the past, Cassie," she said, her voice uncharacteristically cool. "There's really no point in dredging it up."

I wanted to point out that she had no problem dredging up the cat story a moment ago, but something about her demeanor told me to keep my mouth shut. Whatever had happened back then, my mom had clearly been hurt by it. Enough that she still didn't want to think about it twenty years later.

Maybe this really was the scandal everyone claimed it to be.

Two days went by and I was just thinking I was never going to see Jared again when I heard the sound of a revving engine flying my way on Town Line Road. My heart skipped an annoying beat when the engine—whatever it belonged to—sputtered and slowed as it approached the entrance to the ranch's drive. A sleek-looking motorcycle turned up the dirt driveway and even though the driver's face was obscured by a racing helmet, I knew that it was him.

Perfect, I thought sarcastically, looking down at my sweat-stained tank and dirt-streaked arms. *This guy has impeccable timing.*

I was just closing up the stable for the

evening and sweat poured down the back of my neck like a waterfall. It was an unusually hot day for early summer in upstate New York, and considering I had been working my butt off for the last two hours, I was overheated and wilting like a dandelion past its prime. It was definitely the kind of night on which I would normally call Donna and Derek and tell them to meet me at the lake for an evening swim. If only Jared could have shown up *after* I had taken a refreshing, cleansing dip.

No such luck, however. There wasn't much I could do about my appearance in the five seconds it took Jared to fly up the hill to the stable, so I tucked some wet locks of hair behind my ears, pulled my bandanna out of my back pocket, and wiped my face.

Jared killed the engine and pulled off his helmet. Damn if he wasn't even better-looking than I remembered.

"Hey, Gracie," he said with a heart-stopping smile.

"Hi," I replied. "How many vehicles do you actually own?"

"A few," he said, lifting one shoulder.

Like a teenager with multiple autos and cycles and ATVs wasn't a big deal. Yep. He was definitely an invader.

Good. I was glad he had reminded me so quickly. I was still feeling a little miffed over the way he had torn out of the diner the other day. I really didn't want my heart skipping around because of him.

"What are you doing here?" I asked.

"Geez. Blunt much?"

All right. It may have come out even harsher than I intended.

"Just asking a question," I said lightly.

"Yeah, I figured you'd be mad," he said.

"Why would you figure that?"

He dropped the kickstand on his bike and got off, placing his helmet on the seat. He was wearing a white T-shirt that looked impossibly clean in all this heat. In just two days, he was already a lot more tan than he had been the first time I had met him. Obviously someone was taking advantage of the great outdoors he supposedly didn't appreciate.

"Listen, I wanted to apologize," he said, pushing both hands into the back pockets of his jeans. "I was way out of line, ditching you like that after you invited me out."

"Actually, I think you challenged me to take you out," I reminded him.

"Well, whatever," he said, smiling. "I'm sorry. But I just kind of cracked when I heard that girl talking about my mom."

I felt a twinge of regret in my chest. "I know. I'm sorry about that. You just have to understand that your family is kind of legendary around here."

This piqued his interest. "Really?" he said, stepping closer. "My fame precedes me?"

"Not yours, actually. Your parents'," I told him. "We didn't even know *you* existed."

His face fell and I bit my lip to keep from grinning too wide. Score one for the local girl.

"Well, anyway, I probably should've let her explain before I freaked out. I hope we can be friends," he said, offering his hand.

I took it, half reluctantly, half ecstatically. I wasn't at all surprised by the tingle of attraction that raced up my arm when our fingers touched. His grip was firm, but his hands were even softer than mine. Unsurprising considering he'd never held reins, built a fence, or probably even climbed a tree in his life. Poor little rich boy was totally deprived.

But I have to say I was impressed that he had come all the way over here to apologize. As close as the back of his property was to mine, it was a much longer drive from driveway to driveway. And I hadn't expected him ever to acknowledge he might have been wrong, let alone go out of his way to do so. I guess even invaders can surprise you sometimes.

Jared gripped my hand and pulled me toward him with a jerk. I yelped, surprised at being yanked nearly off my feet. Our chests were almost touching as he sniffed dramatically.

"Gracie, you stink," he said in an almost flirtatious way.

I yanked my hand away and kicked some dirt on his pristine black boots. "Gee, thanks," I said, my heart pounding at his proximity. "Some of us have to work for a living."

"Yeah? What do you do, exactly?" he asked, crossing his arms over his chest.

"I give riding lessons," I told him, glancing

over my shoulder at the paddock. "This summer I'm hopefully earning the entry fee for a jumper competition at the county fair in August. I plan to win first prize."

Jared grinned. "I like your confidence."

"Yeah, well, it makes the *stink* worth it," I said.

"I know a good cure for it if you're game. The stink, I mean, not the confidence," he said. "I noticed a beach down by the lake. You hang out there?"

"All the time," I replied.

"Cool. Care to join me?" he said, tilting his head toward his bike.

My pulse raced and I tried not to smile. Me and Jared down by the lake together, going for a sunset swim? Even though every fiber of my being had been raised to be anti-invader, the thought was way too tempting.

Besides, he couldn't be as bad as we all first thought. He had, after all, come to apologize. He wanted to be friends. And I couldn't exactly ignore the fact that I had heart spasms every time he looked at me. I liked that feeling. I had been waiting my entire life to feel that feeling.

"Come on. What do you say?" he prodded.

"Give me five minutes," I told him.

Knowing better than to try to shimmy into my one-piece with my skin covered in sticky sweat (I hadn't worn a bikini since that July Fourth debacle), I blasted myself with the shower quickly and dried off. Bonus? I also got rid of the dirt streaks and stray flecks of manure. All little perks of being a horse nut. I quickly brushed my hair back and fastened it up in a messy bun, then raced to my room to slip on some shorts and throw a few things into my backpack. A brush. A couple of towels—one for me, one for Jared. It took *at least* five minutes just to locate my sunglasses. Somewhere in the middle of all the opening and slamming of drawers, both my parents were drawn to my room by the commotion.

"Why the whirlwind?" my mother asked.

I put my sunglasses on my head, out of breath. "I'm going to the lake."

"With Donna?" my father asked distractedly.

I gulped and looked at my mom. How, exactly, were they going to react to this?

"Um, no. With Jared Kent," I said, holding my breath.

Suddenly Dad was anything but distracted. "Jared Kent?" he repeated, slack-jawed.

"Cassie met him the other day when she was out for her morning ride," my mother explained.

"Let me get this straight. Robert Kent's boy is here? Now?" he asked, pointing at the floor.

Please tell me he's not going to go out there and throw him off the property or something, I thought. *Please don't let him embarrass me.*

"Yeah. He's right outside."

My father turned on his heel and was down the hall in two seconds flat. My mother and I both scurried after him. Dad was generally an enlightened kind of guy. He helped with the dishes and the house cleaning when there wasn't something pressing to be done on the ranch. He had taken me dress shopping when I was a little kid. He had even handled it perfectly when I had gotten my first period and my mom was at

· 73 ·

parent/teacher night half an hour away. Well, as perfectly as a six-foot-four man with four brothers could possibly handle it. But he did love to be a manly-man protector when given the opportunity. That was why part of me was glad I had never met a boy worthy of bringing home. Who knew how Dad would react? Apparently I was about to find out.

"Dad! Come on! We're just going to the lake!" I called after him, my bag slapping up and down on my back.

"Thomas. Don't make a scene," my mother said in a much calmer tone.

My father paused at the front window and looked out. Both my mother and I stopped, stunned. I guess we both assumed he was going right out the door to give Jared the third degree.

"I hope you don't think you're going any-where on that death trap he's got," my father said.

"Dad!"

I was indignant, but also secretly relieved to have an excuse not to get on the motorcycle. After experiencing the way Jared drove his car, I wasn't sure my heart was ready for a two-wheel ride with him.

"Cassie, you'll take the truck," he said.

"Dad, I *am* eighteen years old over here," I said, feeling I needed to take the opportunity to make my point, even though I agreed with him.

"No daughter of mine is ever getting on one of those things," he said, holding the truck keys out to me.

Okay, now the indignation grew. I mean, I loved my dad, but did he really think he was going to be able to tell me what to do forever? We stared at each other over the keys, and for a second, I thought the stalemate would never end, but then my mom dropped onto the couch, knees first like a little kid, and peeked around the curtains.

"So that's Susan's son. Wow. He looks just like his father."

I groaned, took the keys, and glanced past his shoulder. Jared was standing at the open door of the stable, clearly gauging whether or not he should go in and check out the horses.

"Nosy little bugger, isn't he?" my dad said. "Does he not realize he's on private property?"

I rolled my eyes. "All right, I'm going!" I

said, jingling the keys.

"Have fun!" my mom called, looking distressed nevertheless.

"I will!" I replied. Then I may have slammed the door extra hard, just to make some unknown point. Never hurts to slam something now and then when you've lost a standoff. Unless, of course, there's a finger in the way.

I walked out to the truck and started the beleaguered engine. It sputtered and bucked a bit as I made my way down the drive toward Jared and I was sweating all over again by the time I got there. This time out of humiliation.

Jared laughed when he saw me. "We're not taking that thing."

"Yes we are," I said out the window. "I don't do motorcycles."

"Give me a break," he said.

I sighed. "Look, my dad will freak if I get on your bike. He'll either have a heart attack or he'll ground me. I'd rather not have either of those happen."

"Oh. Baby still listening to daddy?" he said with a high-pitched voice.

My cheeks turned crimson. "You know, I'm

starting to really not like you," I lied. It wasn't him I was irritated at, even if he was being irritating. I was more annoyed at myself for letting the father card slip and for not having the guts to just get on the damn motorcycle. "It's the truck or nothing," I told him.

"Wow. You are seriously repressed," he said, walking over to the passenger side. Thanks to his comment, I let him sit right down on the bad spring. "Ow," he complained, sliding aside and checking the butt of his shorts for tears.

"Sorry," I said casually. "And I'm not repressed. I just like my body in one piece."

He ran his eyes over my unrevealing bathing suit, somehow making me feel like I was wearing a string bikini. "So do I," he said waggling his eyebrows in a joking way.

Yeah, I guess I fully set myself up for that one.

"Do you want to go to the beach or not?" I asked, trying not to smile.

"Drive on," he said, leaning toward the door. "But I will get you on my bike before the end of the summer."

I shoved the truck into gear and bucked us

forward, knocking Jared's head against the door. At that moment I understood why he wanted to be the one to drive everywhere. There was a certain power to being the one behind the wheel.

"Yeah," I said with a grin. "That's what *you* think."

Chapter Six

I wasn't at all surprised to see all the familiar cars parked in the lot when we arrived at the lake. Dino Anderson's SUV was there and so was Maureen Mangles's secondhand VW, which meant she and her boyfriend, Gary, were there, among others. My heart started to pound with trepidation as I slammed the door of the pickup. Those guys were not going to take well to my fraternizing with an invader. All I could do was hope that they weren't in a testosterone-y mood. Then there might be some trouble.

"You all right?" Jared asked me.

I stepped over one of the prone logs that acted as a border between the lot and the grass and led him over to the dirt path that wound its way toward the beach. I could already hear the music playing from someone's stereo and a couple of loud whoops and splashes.

"I'm fine. Why?" I asked.

"I don't know. You suddenly look even more ill than you did when you got out of my car the other day," he said with a smile.

I flushed, embarrassed that he had noticed my discomfort. "I'm just looking forward to a swim," I said.

We emerged from the trees and onto the wide, sandy, man-made beach. Sure enough, Maureen, Alison, and a couple of other girls from my class were hanging out on a blanket, flipping through magazines and munching on chips and pretzels. Dino, Gary, Mike, and a few of the guys from the football team were out on the raft, executing flips and cannonballs off the diving board. The dark blue water looked freezing cold, but still inviting. Of course, it would have been more so if those loud-mouthed guys hadn't been taking up so much space.

Out in the distance, on the deeper part of the lake, a pair of small sailboats with pure white sails chased each other westward. A motorboat with a water-skier attached zipped by in the other direction. It looked like water-sport season was officially underway.

"Hi, guys!" I said, the moment Maureen and the others noticed us. They, of course, blatantly checked out Jared. I was pleased to see the look of surprised awe on Alison's face as she leaned over to whisper to Mara Winters.

"Hey." Maureen was the only one who answered. The others were too busy wondering who Jared was and what he was doing with me.

Normally I would have gone over and hung out with them. Maureen was pretty cool and Alison was tolerable when she wasn't sucking face with Dino. But the last thing I wanted to do just then was introduce Jared and spend the next hour listening to them grill him about his family and living in New York City. The benevolent part of me didn't want to put him through it and the more selfish part of me wanted to keep him to myself. Once everyone knew he was a Kent he would develop instant celebrity status and all the good and bad attention that went with it. I kind of wanted to get to know him first.

"Those your friends?" Jared asked as we

laid out our towels a good distance away from them.

"Some of them," I told him.

The guys were swimming toward the water's edge now and I saw Dino eyeing Jared curiously. Jared watched them as they stepped out of the lake and walked dripping wet over to their towels.

"What's up, Cassie?" Mike said, lifting his chin in my direction.

"Hey, Mike," I replied.

He shot Jared a curious look, but said nothing. There was so much manly sizing-each-other-up that I felt like they were about to start circling one another and sniffing each other's butts like dogs. I dropped down on my towel and started rummaging through my bag, trying to ignore all of them.

"You gonna introduce me to any of them?" Jared asked finally.

We both looked over at the beach blankets where every last one of my classmates was clearly talking about me and Jared. Dino smirked in our direction and, although I wasn't sure what it meant, I knew it couldn't be good.

"Probably not a good idea," I said. "Some of the kids don't really like it when out-of-towners hit the local spots."

Jared's chin dropped. "You've gotta be kidding me. What is this, 1955?"

"What's 1955 got to do with anything?" I asked.

"I don't know, turf wars come to mind," Jared said tersely. "Or just a time when people were closed-minded and backward."

Whoa. Was he calling my friends backward? Even if it had a slight pinch of truth, he had no right to say it. He had only been here for less than a week.

"I knew coming up here was a mistake," he said, leaning back on his elbows and staring up at the clear blue sky. "I could be in the Hamptons right now, partying with my friends instead of sitting here getting ostracized by a bunch of country bumpkins."

"Hey!" I protested.

I couldn't let that one slide.

"Hey, Cassie! Is that guy bothering you?" Mike asked, standing up and rolling his sizable shoulders back.

I looked at him and laughed. "Uh, no, Mike. At ease," I joked.

He nodded, looking none too convinced, and dropped back down on the blanket, never taking his eyes off Jared. I guess around Lake Logan we protect our own.

"Sorry," Jared said, pulling a glance at a Mike. "I didn't mean you. It's just . . . man. I can see the boring stretching out in front of me like an eternity."

I sighed. Apparently he didn't even realize that everything he said was hitting me like a personal insult.

"Look, if you don't want to be here, then why are you here?" I asked him, standing up. I dropped my shorts and watched him blatantly check out my legs. Then he looked down and picked up a handful of sand, letting it run through his fingers.

"My dad kind of . . . made me come," he said.

I scoffed. "Sheesh. Who's the baby now?" I said, raising my eyebrows.

He looked up at me, his eyes flashing, but I turned around and strode over to the water before he could make a comeback. Reaching my hands over my head I took two steps into the frigid water, then plunged forward, head first. It was like diving into an ice bucket, but it was exactly what I needed to clear a day of sweat and toil right off of me.

When I resurfaced, Jared was still sitting there, playing with the sand like a petulant child. What was his deal, exactly? Was he the fun-loving daredevil or the pouty kid who hated that he couldn't get his way? Did he want to hang out with me or was he just using me to fill time like Derek had suggested?

I pushed myself onto my back and floated, letting the water fill my ears and envelop me in silence. I watched the wispy clouds high in the sky and sighed. I really didn't know what to think about Jared. Clearly, I was attracted to him. That much I could admit. And hanging out with him would definitely put some excitement in an otherwise predictable summer. But hanging out with him could also cause me some serious trouble—with Derek, with my dad, with the other locals. Trouble I didn't even want to think about.

"Do you think I'm sorority material?" Donna asked from behind her Rutgers University catalog.

Derek launched a kernel of popcorn at me and I expertly caught it in my mouth. We were sitting on the round vinyl bench near the glass doors that fronted the movie theater, all of which were open. Outside it was another scorcher, and after a morning of lessons, I had come over to use the theater for its free popcorn, endless soda supply, and air-conditioning. This was a fairly frequent summer ritual. Unfortunately, this morning, the AC had broken down. Thus the open doors.

"Definitely," Derek said, taking a sip of his soda. "As long as it's the *Animal House* kind and not the *Legally Blonde* kind."

Donna dropped the catalog into her lap. "Hello? *Animal House* was a *fraternity*."

Derek laughed. "Oh. Right. Then no."

She whacked him with the heavy book, which sent him leaning sideways. A warm breeze kicked up, spiraling her red curls all over the place. I whipped an elastic headband out of my back pocket and handed it to her so she could get her hair out of her face. We were always randomly accessorizing each other.

"Don't listen to him," I said, taking the bucket of popcorn from his side. "I think you'd do great in a sorority if you want to be in one. But if you think you need one to make friends, don't. You will have no problem there."

"Thanks," Donna said with a smile. Then she sighed and opened the catalog again. "This place just looks *so* big."

My heart thumped extra hard at the thought of Donna down at Rutgers surrounded by strangers. She would make a new best friend— some perky sorority girl in a cardigan—and they would go to parties together and talk about boys and take the train into New York City. (One of the reasons Donna wanted to go there was because it was close to Manhattan.) What was I supposed to do when I was replaced?

"Why the hell aren't we going to the same school?" Donna asked suddenly, reading my thoughts.

I put my head on her shoulder and sighed. "I have no idea."

Just then a sleek white Lexus pulled into the U Save gas station across the street. The back door opened and out stepped Jared. My whole body started tingling before I even fully registered it was him.

"Oh, look. There's your boy, Cass," Derek teased.

"He's not my boy," I said, even though my pulse rate begged to differ.

An older man with graying hair stepped out from behind the wheel and stretched his arms out at his sides, taking a deep breath of the fresh air.

"Holy crap. That must be his dad. He looks just like him!" Donna said, leaning forward. "My God. We're actually looking at the infamous Robert Kent. He does kind of have a James Bond thing going on, no?"

"Totally," I replied.

I kind of felt like a shameless Peeping Tom, gaping at a clueless Jared as he pumped gas into the tank, but I was pretty much brimming with curiosity. I squinted and tried to get a look at the woman in the passenger seat. Susan Kent. My mother's former best friend. Lake Logan's most famous former resident. I was dying to know what she looked like, but she was mostly in shadow and all I could make out was a head of poofy blond hair. She flipped the visor down and checked her lipstick in the mirror. I saw her reapply and press her lips together before sitting back in the seat, satisfied.

"I wish *she* would get out of the car," Donna said.

"What's the big deal? She's just a woman," Derek put in, though he was watching just as closely as we were.

Jared's father went inside the little gas station to pay and Jared leaned against the driver's side door, his legs crossed at the ankle. He tipped his head back, yawned, and drummed his fingers against the car. When his dad came back he jumped to attention and held the car door while his father slowly lowered himself into the seat. Then he slammed it, got in the back, and the Kents drove off.

For a guy who resented his father for dictating his summer plans, Jared sure was helpful to the man. He was almost acting like he was his father's valet.

"Well, I suppose you two are going to dissect *that* sighting for the next two hours," Derek joked.

I glanced at my watch. "Actually, I have to get home," I said, handing him the bucket of popcorn. "New clients coming in at three. Don't want to be late."

"Aw, really?" Donna whined.

"Sorry, kids. I'll call you tonight," I said, pushing open the door.

"There she goes! Reliable, predictable Cassie Grace!" Derek called out as I stepped into the thick, humid afternoon.

I shot him a look of death as his comment got right under my skin. Why did it seem that lately, the jab that I'd been hearing most of my life was getting to me more than usual?

Chapter Seven

"Josh! You have to sit still in the saddle!" I ordered, trying with all my strength to keep from losing my head. "Stop squirming! You're going to freak her out and then she'll run and if she runs you'll fall and if you fall, well, then we're both pretty much dead."

Actually, Miss Piggy, being an old and untemperamental nag, had long since become unfreakable. That was what a few years of lessons with rambunctious kids could do to an aging horse. But in my experience it didn't do any harm to threaten idly.

Josh Locke, angel that he was, reached into the pocket of his jeans, pulled out a handful of dirt, and threw it in my face. I had just enough time to close my eyes to keep from being blinded, but I did get a nice big taste of it on my tongue. Both Josh and his older brother, Seth, cracked up laughing.

Still clinging to Piggy's reins, I bent over and spit repeatedly onto the ground, coughing and sputtering and working my tongue to try to keep from swallowing the dirt.

"All right! That's it! The lesson is over," I said, reaching up.

Josh slid toward me and let me deposit him on the ground. Then he ran off to race around the training ring with his brother, throwing mud at each other as they went. In the center of the ring was a nice pile of dung that Piggy had left halfway through our lesson. All I could hope was that one of the little monsters would shove the other into it.

I walked Miss Piggy over to the fence where Lola was tied up, watching the proceedings and flicking flies with her tail. There was a bottle of water in my backpack hanging from the post, so I rinsed out my mouth a few times and wiped my hand across my lips. I sighed and leaned next to my horse.

"Is this really worth it, Lola?" I asked.

She snorted and nudged the top of my head with her snout. The girl had a point. If I didn't do this, I was never going to make the money for our entry fee for the county fair. Then Lola would never get her blue ribbon and I would never get my book and food and fun money. I rubbed her snout and shook my hair back.

"Anything for you, kid," I told her, giving her a quick kiss.

The two boys screeched and raced toward the gate. It wasn't until then that I noticed their mother's shiny black auto winding its way up the drive. Sweet relief. The devil was here to pick up her minions.

"Mommy! Mommy! Mommy!" Josh shouted, jumping up and down as she got out of the car. This one was even worse than Shelby's mom. She wore a tight white mini-dress and white heels, her hair pulled back in a severe bun, making her pointy face appear even more sharp.

I opened the gate and her two sons ran toward her, arms outstretched. Mrs. Locke's jaw dropped and she held out both hands like stop signals, bending at the knee.

"Stop! Right! There!" she shouted.

Amazingly, the little terrors did as they were told. First time that had happened all day long.

"Cassandra Grace! Why are my boys covered in mud?" she asked, wrinkling her nose.

"Well, Mrs. Locke, unfortunately they were more interested in having a mud fight than they were in riding," I said, trying to smile as though I thought this was amusing.

"This is unacceptable!" she snapped. "When I left my sons in your care I expected you to actually *care* for them."

"I did my best," I told her, my face beginning to burn. "But your children clearly have no interest in horses."

"And isn't that your job?" she asked, folding her slim arms over her chest. "To get them interested in horses?"

My face started to burn and my tongue twisted into knots. My toes curled in frustration inside my boots. I knew that she was wrong. I knew that I had a perfectly legitimate beef with these kids, but I couldn't think of a single thing to say. Whenever an adult confronted me, I lost the ability to speak. No matter how hard I tried or how in the right I was, I could never ever defend myself.

The woman smirked, clearly enjoying the fact that she had beaten me into submission. And it hadn't even taken that much effort.

Say something, Cassie! Come on! a little voice in my mind squealed. *You hold your own with Jared! Defend yourself to this lizard-looking woman, too!*

But I couldn't. I looked at the ground and blew out an irritated sigh.

"The next time I come here to pick up my children, I expect them to be clean and ready to go," Mrs. Locke said. "Come on, boys. I'll put a blanket down for you in the backseat. We'll be back here on Saturday morning for their next lesson," she said over her shoulder.

"Saturday? But I thought—"

"I already made arrangements with your father," she said. "That will be their regular lesson time."

I bit my tongue and looked at the ground. Saturday wasn't a problem for me, but I couldn't believe my father had just made arrangements for a regular lesson without even asking if the timing was okay. Was I a paid instructor or a slave?

As the Lockes headed for their car, Marni kept a good three feet between her precious white dress and her sons. She removed a plaid blanket from the trunk and carefully covered the tan leather interior of her car before letting her kids anywhere near it. Some life those nutcases must have. Even though they had tortured me for the last hour, I almost felt sorry for them.

Almost.

"You don't have to give them lessons if they're going to make you miserable," my mother pointed out, opening the door of the Wonder Mart by backing through it. We each had two bags of groceries in our arms and it was just starting to rain.

"Yeah, except Dad already set it all up," I pointed out.

"Cassie, he only did it because he thought you would be fine with it," she said patiently. "All you've talked about for months is taking on more lessons and making that entry fee. He was just thinking of you."

"I know," I said, chagrined. "You're right. I need the money. I'll just have to be patient." I said, glancing up at the cloud-covered sky.

"That's my girl," my mother said.

Reliable. Predictable, I added silently.

As we reached her car, the first fat raindrops plopped from the sky, smacking against the overheated asphalt. I sighed in relief as a cool breeze blew a few more drops over my neck and face. A nice, big, humidity-breaking thunderstorm was exactly what we needed around here.

My mother popped open the trunk and the rain started to come down in earnest. We threw our paper bags inside and slammed it, screeching and laughing as we struggled with the car doors. By the time we got inside, my hair and T-shirt were soaked and sticking to my skin. Just like that. Five seconds and we had a downpour on our hands.

"Love a summer storm," my mother said with a sigh. Somewhere off in the distance, thunder rumbled. The green leaves on the trees turned upside down in the wind and the road was already slick.

She started the engine and put on the wipers and lights. I loved the soothing *pock-pock* sound of the windshield wipers as they methodically slapped the rain aside. Like my mother, I always found a good thunderstorm soothing.

Mom inched the car toward the exit, then paused. "I can barely see through the windshield," she said. "Maybe we should wait until it lets up a bit."

"Sounds like a plan," I replied, settling in.

Mom pulled into the last space in the lot and we sat back to wait. I heard another rumble of thunder, but then quickly realized it wasn't thunder at all. I glanced at my mother and we both looked up at the wet road. Suddenly, a car zoomed by, zig-zagging down the two-way street in the rain. I recognized the auto instantly, even before I heard the sound of Jared's voice cheering through the rain.

"Was that . . . ?" my mother said.

"Oh yeah," I replied, swallowing with difficulty.

Seconds later, another car sped by, chasing

after Jared. Then a third. All three were all over the road and all three were driven by whooping boys who couldn't possibly have been paying attention to what they were doing. Apparently, Jared's friends from the city had arrived. And apparently, his summer of eternal boredom was over.

"Don't they realize how dangerous that is?" my mother said. "The roads are as slick as ice at the beginning of a storm."

"I know," I said, my heart in my throat. I just hoped Jared wouldn't do anything stupid. Well, more stupid than what he was already doing.

"Well, now I'm glad your father didn't let you get on that kid's motorcycle the other day," my mother said. "Clearly he's a little out of control."

"He's just having some fun, Mom," I said automatically.

"Cassie, please tell me you wouldn't get into the car with him if he was going to do something like this," she said, her jaw slack. "He'll be lucky if he doesn't wrap that car of his around a tree."

"I wouldn't," I said. "Just, I don't know, try

not to judge him so quickly."

My mom exhaled and smiled, tilting her head and looking at me like I was a little girl. "Well, just be careful when you're with him, all right? For my sake."

"I will," I told her, fastening my own seat belt as the rain slowed down a bit. *If I ever even hear from him again, now that his buddies are in town,* I added silently.

Three days later, I lay in bed, staring at the ceiling and listening to the chorus of crickets outside my window. I couldn't sleep. Jared hadn't called, hadn't stopped in, hadn't so much as NASCAR-ed by my house since I had seen him in the rain.

The longer I went without seeing him, the more I couldn't stop thinking about him. Half my thoughts were angry ones. After all, it looked like he really *had* been using me to pass the time until his real friends showed up. And I, like an idiot, had just let it happen, thinking everyone else was wrong. That there was some kind of connection between us.

But the other half of my thoughts were,

well, more like daydreams. Daydreams that he would show up at my house in the middle of the night and throw pebbles at my window. That we would go for a walk in the moonlight and he would tell me what an idiot he had been—that I was the exciting one and his Manhattan friends were the boring ones. Then he would slip his hand under my hair and I would tilt my face up to his. Under the stars our lips would meet and it would be the most knee-weakening kiss of all time, worthy of the big screen. He would take me in his arms and pick me up and—

I sat up straight in bed, short of breath and every inch of my skin humming. Enough was enough. I had to get out of here before my imagination took over and I lost all sense of reality.

I whipped my sheets aside and walked over to the window and looked out. Nothing. Nothing but the empty fields and the leaves rustling in the breeze. He wasn't coming over to sweep me off my feet. Just staring at my yard, I was seized by an all-encompassing disappointment. This was what I had become. This was what happened when you lived in a town where nothing interesting ever happened. You found yourself crushed when your psychotic daydreams turned out to be just that. You found yourself saddened to see that your yard was, in fact, unpeopled in the middle of the damn night. It was time to get a grip.

I pulled on a pair of jeans and a T-shirt from the floor, added some socks, and yanked on my favorite cowboy boots. Tucking my hair under my battered New York Yankees cap, I grabbed a flashlight and headed out. A little ride under the stars with Lola would clear my head.

Lola was surprised to see me, but didn't protest when I led her out of her stall and saddled her up. It had been a long time since my last midnight ride—this past fall when I was waiting to hear back from colleges. Back then, there had definitely been a few sleepless nights, but I had been fine all winter, which was good, considering both Lola and I would have frozen to death if I had taken her out in January.

Once I was mounted, I leaned down and stroked her mane. "Don't worry," I whispered. "I'm not losing it. At least I don't think I am."

I gave her a little nudge and we walked out of the stable and into the night. I wasn't feeling the need for speed—just a little relaxing ride—so we strolled down the drive and out onto Town Line Road. Usually I had no fear of cars, as Lake Logan was pretty much the city that *always* slept, but after seeing Jared and his friends' antics first hand, I kept my ears trained on the night sounds. If I heard even the smallest hint of an engine, I was getting Lola off the road faster than you could say "lawsuit."

The clouds from the other day had long since cleared and the vast sky was bright with stars and a low-hanging moon. There were no streetlights in Lake Logan, but tonight we didn't need one. I could even make out the striations of bark on the trees as we made our way toward the lake.

I took a deep breath and listened to the sound of Lola's hoofs clopping against the road. So soothing. Yeah, this was what I needed. Serenity. Peace. I could practically fall asleep right here.

We reached the entrance to the lake parking lot and I clucked my tongue at Lola, tugging the reins to the left. She turned and crossed the road, picking up her feet a bit as she realized we were going down by the water. That Lola. Always up for a nice long drink.

I was just about to take her toward the path to the lake, when I saw a car parked at the far end of the lot. Who would be out here at this hour? It was a little late for a swim.

"Whoa," I said, pulling back on the reins. Lola stopped and I squinted into the night. My heart skipped a beat when I realized it was Jared's car. And Jared himself was sitting on the ground behind it, his back propped against the back bumper.

What the. . . ?

"Come on, girl," I said, nudging Lola around.

We cantered over to the car and Lola sniffed haughtily when she got a good look at Jared. Not that I could blame her. He was half slumped over and clearly trashed. Empty beer cans littered the ground all around his car and into a few other empty spaces. He didn't even look up when we stopped a few feet away.

"Hey! Are you alive?" I said, dropping to the ground.

He blinked, took a second to focus, then raised his arms as if for a hug. "Gracie!" he said with a grin. "You gonna drive me home?"

Then he burped.

I cracked an amused smile, then quickly wiped it off my face. This wasn't cute, it was totally lame. Lame, Cassie. Lame.

"Uh, no," I said, clinging to Lola's reins. "Have you been drinking and driving?"

"No!" he cried indignantly. He groped for the car behind him and pressed his hand into its bumper, then hoisted himself unsteadily to his feet. "No! I wouldn't *do* that," he said, wavering. "I drove here. *Sober*. And *then* me and my friends had some beers. And *then* they went out to get some more beers. And *then* they never came back."

He sat back against the closed trunk of his car, looking overly forlorn. I found myself smiling again. I couldn't help it. Why did he have to be so cute?

"Some friends," I said.

"I know! Right?" he said, wide-eyed. "Anyway, you hafta drive me home. I really need to get home."

"Jared, I can't drive you home," I said. "What am I supposed to do with Lola?"

Jared swung his chin up and opened his eyes even wider, trying to focus again. It was as if he had just noticed for the first time that Lola was there. Unreal. She was kind of hard to miss.

"Jus' tie her up. Where's she gonna go?" Jared said.

I rolled my eyes. "Yeah. That's gonna happen."

I walked over to the open door to his car, letting the reins go slack a bit, and checked inside. Just as I remembered. His car was a manual.

"Besides, I can't drive stick," I told him.

Jared looked at me and started to cackle. He bent over at the waist and slapped his hand against his thigh as he laughed. Clearly this was the funniest thing he had ever heard in his life.

My cheeks burned and I was glad it was dark and he was drunk so that my new complexion would go unnoticed.

"Jared!" I said. He kept laughing. "Hey! Jared! Jared Kent! Paging Jared Kent!" I sang, snapping my fingers in front of his face.

Finally he quieted and looked up, only letting out the occasional giggle. "Yeah?"

"Do you want to get home or not?" I asked.

"Wull yeah! But how?" he asked, spreading his arms wide.

I stepped aside so he could see Lola's saddle. "Come on, lush face," I said, smirking as his jaw dropped. "We're going for a ride."

Chapter Eight

It took five tries to get Jared into the saddle. As he kept repeating over and over, he had never ridden a horse before. Between his total lack of experience and his drunken state, he had a hard time lifting his leg over Lola's back. Then, the first time he *did* manage to swing all the way up, he slid over and fell down off the other side. You could break something doing that, but Jared just laughed until he cried.

Finally, I got him up and reasonably steady. With some serious contortion, I climbed up in front of him, fully aware that my butt was directly in his face while I tried to position myself. Burning with humiliation, I sat down and just hoped he was so drunk he wouldn't remember any of this in the morning.

"Hold on to me," I told him.

"Ooh. Now we're getting frisky," he joked.

I rolled my eyes and he hooked his arms around my waist. This was not the best way to ride with a completely uncoordinated novice. I had thought about riding behind him, like I would do with a little kid who had no idea how to control a horse, but it was out of the question. I never would have been able to see past his bulky frame. We were just going to have to roll the dice and hope he didn't loll off the back or slide off the side.

"Jared, just try to stay awake, okay?" I said over my shoulder. "I don't want to lose you."

"Who knew you were such a flirt, Gracie?" Jared asked, blowing his breath directly up my nose. Majorly sour.

"Yeah. That's me. I love a sloppy drunk," I told him. "Come on Lola," I urged, clucking my tongue a couple of times. She grunted, irritated over the added weight, but started us on our way. Suddenly the lazy rhythm of her clip-clopping hooves wasn't so soothing anymore. It was downright annoying. All it did was remind me of how slow we were moving and how far we had to travel.

"I like being this close to you," Jared said, slumping into my back.

My heart skipped a beat and my hands started to sweat, even though it was kind of a cool night. How could I possibly be so excited and so grossed out by the same person at the same time? He smelled like the basement of the VFW and he was more limp than a new balloon, but still, when he said that, my blood raced.

"That's nice," I said, wishing I could truthfully say the same.

"You hate me," he said, sounding like a little kid.

"No I don't," I protested.

"Yeah, you do. You hate me 'cuz I'm from the city," he said, lifting his chin. "And now you hate me because you think I'm a drunk. But I'm not normally like this. It was my friends. They said we had to get drunk 'cuz there was nothing else to do."

I sighed loudly. "And do you always do what your friends want to do?"

"Not always," he said, then laughed. "But it seemed like a good idea at the time."

I smiled. I couldn't help it. There was something cute about the goofy way he was acting. So unlike the "I'm-too-cool" demeanor he usually had going. Plus it was a lot better than the angry or hostile drunk some of the guys from my class displayed when they had their drink on.

"But now you think I'm a jerk," he said, slumping again.

"Not really," I said patiently.

"Well, I'm sorry you have to drive me home. Or horse me home or whatever," he said, causing me to snort a laugh. "You know, you shouldn't be mad at me. If you wanna be mad at someone, be mad at my dad. We wouldn't even be here if it wasn't for him."

"Right. You mentioned that," I said.

We turned off Town Line Road onto Murphy Street, which was even darker and thicker with trees. I gazed into the night and prayed that I wouldn't see headlights. Not that it was very likely. There was absolutely zero to do around here once the Irish pub in Morganville closed down at midnight. Still, I did know pretty much everyone in town and if someone saw us, I was going to have a hard time explaining what I was doing with a drunken invader on the back of my horse in the middle of the night. The driveway to Jared's house was about a half a mile up on the right. The driveway itself was another half mile long. Lola and I were going to have to go back at a trot if I wanted to get to bed before the hour became obscene.

"He's just doing it 'cuz they told him to, though," Jared continued matter-of-factly. "Like me. I'm just doing it 'cuz *he* told *me* to. No one does what they actually *want* to do anymore. You know?"

My brow creased and I glanced over my shoulder at him. "You do know you're not making a whole lot of sense right now, right?"

"No way! No! I'm making perfect sense," he said gesturing with his arm. The second he let go of my waist, he almost fell out of the saddle again. He had to grab onto me hard to keep from going over. My insides lurched in fear, but we stayed upright. "Whoa. That was close."

"Yep," I said, trying not to betray my panic. Just a little bit farther. . . .

"Well, anyway, he says he doesn't want to talk about it, so I said fine. But really it's not fine. Because if you do something that changes your entire life and your whole family's life, you should be able to talk about it, you know?" Jared said.

Now I was thoroughly confused. What the heck was he talking about? Who had told his father to do what? And what had he done to change his whole family's life? So they were here for the summer and not in the Hamptons. Big deal. It was one summer.

"You know, Jared, maybe we should try to keep quiet the rest of the way home," I suggested. "It *is* kind of late."

Jared looked around like he was going to wake up someone sleeping on the side of the road. "Oh, yeah. Shhhhh!" he said in an exaggerated way.

I sighed and tried not to count the clip-clops of Lola's hooves all the way up the winding drive and around the circular fountain to the front door of the Kent mansion. Aside from the old-fashioned standing lamp at the top of the walk, there wasn't a single light on anywhere on the property.

"Oh, hey! We're here!" Jared said.

I felt him move and grabbed his wrist. "Oh no. Allow me," I said.

I swung my leg over Lola's neck and jumped down face-first—a total no-no, but the only way I could dismount without Jared going first. Then I reached up and helped him down, just like I had done with five-year-old Josh Locke the other day. The moment he hit the ground he tripped forward, falling into me. Once again my heart did the pitter-patter dance, but when I smelled his breath again, I put a stop to the insanity.

"Thanks again," Jared said. "I'll call ya."

"Great," I told him.

He was looking at me all gooey-eyed and suddenly I was afraid he might kiss me. I side-stepped him quickly and mounted Lola. The last thing I wanted was to find out what his mouth tasted like at that moment. Probably not a good tactile memory for a girl's first kiss.

"Good night!" I said.

He lifted his hand in an unsteady wave, and I took Lola down the hill as fast as we could go without endangering ourselves in the dark.

Jared Kent was cute. There was no denying that. But as of now, he was on strike three. Or was it four? It was getting difficult to keep track. Either way, as Lola and I made our way home I felt that one thing was for sure. My little foray into the land of the invaders had officially come to a close.

The next night my parents and I gathered at the kitchen table for dinner—pasta with sauce from a jar. I knew my mom had had a long day on the ranch when she served up sauce from a jar. Normally she took a lot of pride in the fact that she cooked pretty much everything from scratch. But this was normal for this time of year. At the beginning of every summer, my mom threw herself into chores on the ranch that she neglected all school year and ended up working herself to the bone for about a week— until she remembered that she had all summer to get everything done.

"Sorry about this," she said, dropping a plate of formerly frozen garlic toast on the table. "I know it doesn't look too appetizing."

My father spread his napkin in his lap and smiled. "It looks amazing, Sweets."

My mom blushed and I gagged, but smiled. It both grossed me out and made me happy when my dad called my mom by his nickname for her. Grossed out because, well, who wants to think about *why* their dad calls their mom "Sweets"? Happy because it was nice to have parents who still genuinely liked each other. Not all of my friends were so lucky.

"Well, dig in," my mother told us, setting a salad in the center of the table.

A breeze blew the curtains in from outside and at the same moment, we all heard a car pulling up the driveway. My father crunched into some garlic bread. My mom glanced at me quizzically, then turned to look out the front kitchen window.

"Cassie, I think you have a visitor," she said coyly.

Dad stopped chewing. My heart flip-flopped. We both knew that if it was one of the Policastros, she just would have said so and set out another plate. A car door slammed. Footsteps crunched up the front walk. Still, for some reason when the doorbell rang, I was startled.

"I guess I'll get it," I said, pushing my chair away from the table.

At the door, I inched the plaid curtain aside and caught a glimpse of Jared's profile. Model perfect. Suddenly dry in the mouth, I let the curtain fall back and took a deep breath. My nerves jangled like Christmas bells. What the heck was he doing here? And didn't he know it was dinner time?

"Cassie? Who is it?" my father called.

With all the open windows, Jared had definitely heard that. Snagged. I held my breath and opened the door.

"Hi!" I said casually. He was holding a bunch of wildflowers wrapped in a white paper towel. "What's that?"

"A lame apology?" Jared said, holding them out. "You guys don't have a florist around here, huh?"

"Yeah. It's just a couple towns over," I said, taking the flowers. "But thanks, these are beautiful." It actually looked as if he had put some thought into the arrangement—yellows in the center, purples all around. Of course, I had never gotten flowers from a guy before in my life. He could have handed me a fistful of dandelions and I would have been touched. So much for writing him off. Who knew I was such a pushover?

"Oh. I'll have to remember that," he said.

Like he was going to be giving me flowers again sometime.

"So, listen, thanks for last night," Jared said, scratching at the back of his neck as he avoided my direct gaze, clearly embarrassed. "I can't even remember most of what I said, but I'm guessing it wasn't good."

"No. You were totally fine," I lied. "Besides, I pick up drunks on my horse all the time. Lola and I are the designated drivers of Lake Logan."

Jared laughed. "Well, you guys are good Samaritans," he said. "I'm just sorry you had to see me like that."

"Is this going to turn into a habit?" I asked him, raising my eyebrows. "You doing something stupid, then showing up at my house to apologize?"

Jared's jaw dropped slightly and he took a

step back, his blue eyes dancing. "Wow. You slay me with your words!"

"Just calling 'em like I see 'em," I said with a little smile.

"Well, I hope it's not gonna be a habit," he said, smiling back. "I've decided, after having to walk back to the lake this morning in the burning sun to pick up my car and then searching for the keys, which I apparently threw into the trees as some kind of display of my pitching prowess, that I am turning over a new leaf."

"Really?" I said with a laugh. "This I gotta see."

"No! I swear. In fact, that's why I want to ask you out to dinner," Jared said matter-of-factly. "I heard there's a restaurant in Washingtonville. A real one. Something Italian . . . ?"

"Raimundo's," I told him.

He snapped his fingers. "Yes, that's it. I'd like you take you there. Tonight. Now, if you're free."

"What are you kidding?" I said. Raimundo's on a Tuesday night? With no planning? No reservation? No getting dressed up and coiffed and leaving half an hour early to make sure we got there in time?

That sort of sounded like something an *un*predictable person would do.

"Do I look like I'm kidding?" he replied, stepping back so I could get a good look at his outfit. He wore baggy but unwrinkled chinos and a white linen shirt. Dressed up by Lake Logan standards. "I think this whole effort barely suffices as an apology-slash-thank you." He looked at me hopefully and when I didn't move, he leaned toward me and lowered his voice. "Plus my mom fired our cook, which means she's making dinner herself tonight so really, you'd be saving me all over again."

He bit his lip and it nearly sent my heart into overdrive. This boy really did know how to make an offer.

I took a deep breath and glanced over my shoulder. My parents were whispering intently in the kitchen. I could practically *feel* my father getting restless and curious.

This was going to be an interesting conversation. "Just . . . hang on one sec," I said, holding up a finger. "I'm going to go put these in some water."

"I got nowhere else to go," Jared said, spreading his arms wide.

I closed the door on him and steeled myself. For some reason, I had a feeling my father wasn't going to be too happy with my request. The best thing to do would be to put it to him in a way that he couldn't refuse. Make it seem like there wasn't anything wrong with walking out on dinner with the family to go out with an invader. Nothing strange about me going to a fancy restaurant with a boy I had just met. Yeah. That was the ticket.

I shook my hair back and walked confidently into the kitchen, my heart pounding. "I'm going out to Raimundo's with Jared," I said with a smile. It's really hard to smile when my stomach is revolting from nerves.

My father's face went white. "Pardon me?"

"He wants to check it out," I told my dad, grabbing a vase out of the cabinet under the sink. My hand was shaking as I held it under the water. "You don't mind, do you, Mom?"

My mother looked from my father to the food on the table and shrugged. "Well, it's not as if I went to much trouble. . . ."

"No. I'm sorry, but Cassie, he just came up here and interrupted our dinner without so much as a phone call," my father said firmly. "You're not rewarding him for that kind of behavior with a date."

Damn, my father could be seriously old-school. I put the flowers in the vase and set them next to the sink. Then I took a deep breath and turned to look at my dad.

"It's not a date," I said, wondering whether or not this was true. "I'm just trying to help him out. Show him around. You're always saying how ridiculous it is—the line between us and the invaders. I'm just trying to be friendly."

The last thing I was going to do was admit that the invite was actually a thank you for giving him a ride home in the middle of the night. That would not go over well. My father sighed and looked down at his plate.

"Come on, Thomas. It's just one dinner," my mother chided.

My father shook his head like he couldn't believe what he was about to say. "Fine. Go. But be back early."

I jumped and rushed over to give my dad a

kiss on the cheek. Part of me was certain that I would have walked out even if he *had* said no — just to assert my eighteen-year-old-ness — but I was glad I didn't have to test it.

"Thanks, guys!"

I ran to my room, stripped out of my clothes, and threw on the sundress I had worn under my gown at graduation. After dotting on some lip gloss, I took a second to grin at my reflection in the mirror, savoring the moment. My first maybe-date. This summer was already ten times more exciting than I could have ever predicted.

Chapter Nine

I sat in my chair at Raimundo's and watched Jared over the top of my menu. Ever since we were ushered to our table, he had been scanning the room—sizing it up. Probably comparing it to all the swank restaurants and cool hangouts he frequented in the city. I glanced around and tried to see what he was seeing as if for the first time. The white tablecloths. The dark walls. The votive candles flickering on the tables. Was it as elegant to him as it was to me? Or was all of this "so five minutes ago"?

"So? What do you think?" I asked him, closing my menu and setting it aside.

"It's nice," he said with a thoughtful frown.

"Not what you're used to, though. Right?" I asked.

"Oh, no. I mean, there are a million places like this in the city," he said.

The upstate girl in me immediately took this as an insult. Raimundo's was the nicest restaurant we had for miles, but to him it was a dime a million. I took a deep breath and told myself to chill. After all, he wasn't *trying* to be critical. He was just from a whole different world.

"The food does smell amazing," he said, taking a deep breath and smiling.

Okay, he was forgiven. And damn, did he look good by candlelight.

The waiter came over and took our order—chicken parmagiana for me, mussels marinara for Jared with an antipasto appetizer—and then we fell into an awkward silence. He looked at me. I smiled and quickly glanced away. I looked at him. He cleared his throat and stared at his water glass, running his fingers up and down its sides to clear the condensation. Hushed conversations and light laughter continued all around us and I felt like it was mocking me. Everyone else had something to talk about. Why not us?

All right, just say something, I willed myself. *This is Jared Kent. There are probably about a zillion and one things you can ask him.*

"So, what would you be doing right now if you were back in the city?" I asked him, leaning my elbows on the table. If there was one thing even I knew about boys, it was that they *loved* to talk about themselves.

Jared sat up a little straighter. "What would I be doing . . . ?" he said, narrowing his eyes and rubbing his hands together. "Actually, my night probably wouldn't get started for at least another hour."

"Really? You guys eat late, huh?" I said.

"Yeah. Me and my friends would probably hit one of the restaurants on the East Side and have some food. Hang out for a while if there's a game on or if there's a scene," he said, clearly warming to his subject. "Then we'd probably—"

"I'm sorry. Go back for a sec," I said. "What qualifies as 'a scene'?"

"Oh, you know, it depends on whether there are any hot wo—"

Jared looked at me and flushed. I flushed right back.

"Not that I pick up a lot of women or anything," Jared said quickly. "I don't. Not like my friends do. But having girls with you makes it easier to get into the clubs." He cleared his throat again, looking sheepish.

I laughed. "Wait a minute, wait a minute. You, Jared Kent, have trouble getting into clubs?"

He bit his bottom lip. "No, actually. We're on the VIP lists pretty much everywhere." He leaned forward, forearms on the table and laid some serious puppy dog eyes on me. "Listen, I don't want you to get the wrong idea. I'm not some maniac womanizer or something. My friends and I just like to have fun."

My heart skipped a beat at the way he was looking into my eyes. Like he truly needed to make me understand—to win me over. "Why is it so important to you that I not get the wrong idea?" I asked.

He blinked and looked down at the table. The moment was broken, but my skin still sizzled. "I don't know. It just is."

"So that's what you do for fun on a Tuesday night? Go out and get trashed with your friends and a bunch of random women?" I asked.

"See! I *knew* you were going to get the wrong

idea," he said, lifting a hand and then slumping back. "I mean, it's not like there's anything else to do."

"What?" I blurted out so loud that people at all the surrounding tables fell quiet and gaped at me. But, hey, I was that surprised. "It's New York City," I said, lowering my voice. "You've got museums and Broadway shows and off-Broadway plays and music halls and jazz clubs and who knows what else? I would kill to have that many options."

"Spoken like a true tourist," Jared said teasingly.

"I'm just saying. You don't know bored until you've lived in Lake Logan your whole life," I told him.

Jared raised his eyebrows. "Whoa, whoa, whoa. Little Miss Lake Logan has problems with her town? The girl who almost tore my head off for suggesting that life here might not be all that interesting? What happened?"

Oops. Snagged. I squirmed in my seat, embarrassed. "Look, *I* can mock the place all I want. I live here. It's when you invaders make these snap judgments about us that everyone thinks—"

"Invaders?" Jared said.

My jaw dropped slightly. What was *wrong* with me tonight? A Lake Loganer *never* called a summer local an invader to his face. Unless she was itching for a fist fight. Not that I thought Jared would deck me or something, but I knew he would probably be offended. Plus it was like I had betrayed my people—let one of the outsiders in on our special lingo.

"What?" I said, trying to play stupid.

"What's an invader?" he asked, intrigued.

"Nothing! Forget it. It's just a joke," I said. The waiter pushed through the kitchen door with a plate full of meat, cheese, and veggies and placed it on our table. "Oooh! That looks good!" I said, hoping to change the subject.

"Gracie, come on. What's an invader?" he said. "Tell me. I can keep a secret."

It was always the people who claimed they could keep secrets who ended up blabbing everything all over the place. I took a deep breath and picked up a piece of cheese. Clearly

Jared was not going to let this drop. Who could blame him? If someone had called me something like that, I would want to know why.

"All right, fine," I said, swallowing hard. "It's what we call the summer locals. 'Invaders.' I think it came from that old video game Space Invaders? Somebody started it back in the eighties or something and eventually it just got shortened to invaders. You know, 'cuz you guys come up here every summer and invade our space."

Jared just stared at me for a second and I was positive he was going to get up and storm right out, offended that we had a generalizing nickname for him and his friends. Instead, he cracked up laughing.

"That's pretty good," he said, popping a black olive into his mouth. "I like it. Invaders. I have to tell my mom that."

I nibbled on my cheese, relieved. "She might already know about it," I said. "After all, she did still live here in the eighties, right?"

Jared considered this for a second. "Yeah, I guess you're right. It's still so weird to think of my mom living here. She was born to live in the city."

"Well, she is one of the few who got out of here and stayed out," I said with a sigh.

"Envious, are we?" Jared asked, taking a bite of prosciutto.

I took a sip of my water, stalling. Apparently, Jared had already figured out how to read me. Was I that transparent or was he just that good?

"Don't get me wrong. I love this town," I said. "But I *am* looking forward to getting out of here for a while. You have no idea how freeing it would be to be able to walk down the street without someone stopping me to ask how my history test went or whether one of our horses had her foal yet. I mean, everyone knows *everything*."

"They can't know *everything*," Jared said.

"Tomorrow, walk around town and ask any person you see how long it took for me to get my braces off," I told him. "Trust me. They know."

"You had braces?" Jared asked. "Nah. I don't believe that."

"Why?"

"Your smile is totally perfect."

I grinned automatically, then slapped my hand over my mouth in case he thought I was fishing for more compliments. "That is kind of the point of braces," I said through my fingers.

"Good point, but it is! Seriously. Let me see," Jared said, reaching over and pulling my hand down. When our fingers hit the table, he held my hand there, pressing it lightly to the tablecloth. My pulse went berserk. Was he holding my hand? Was he actually holding my hand?

"Yeah," he said, staring at my out-of-control smile. "Perfect."

"Well after three and a half years in those things, it better be," I said.

Somehow I managed to look him in the eye. It took pretty much every ounce of willpower and courage I had in my body, but I did it. His half smile sent shivers all down my spine. I never wanted to stop holding his hand. I never wanted him to stop looking at me that way.

I was in big trouble.

Chapter Ten

*B*y the time we got home it was pitch black outside. Clouds had rolled in and blocked out the moon and stars and thickened the night air to the point where I could feel it clinging to me as Jared walked me to the door. My stomach was full to bursting, and considering how hard I had worked and how much I had eaten, I should have been about ready to pass out. Instead, my heart was pounding and every inch of my body was awake and alert.

I was going to get my first kiss. I was sure of it. And could I ask for a better moment? Dinner alone at a nice restaurant. An incredible talk over candlelight. A leisurely drive home with no daredevil moves whatsoever. And Jared. Jared Kent who was far more exciting, far more interesting, far more gorgeous than any other guy I had ever met. No wonder my blood was rushing so fast.

"So, am I forgiven?" Jared asked as we paused at my front door. The light was on over the steps, but there was no sign of my parents.

"Forgiven?" I asked, smiling in an admittedly loopy way. I swear I felt drugged or something. It made me wonder whether pasta had hidden endorphins. More likely it was just being around Jared—wondering what would happen next.

"For last night," he said.

"Oh! Right!" I exclaimed. I had completely forgotten that this night had started out as an apology. "Yes. You are definitely forgiven."

"Buy a girl a little Italian food and you can get away with anything," Jared joked, taking a step closer to me.

"You are a master of the female mind, Jared Kent," I joked back.

"So," he said, reaching out and taking my hand.

I took one small step closer to him. The skirt of my dress brushed the front of his pants. "So . . ."

He searched my eyes, smiled, and leaned slowly toward me. Exhilarated panic seized my heart. This was it! What should I do? Close my lips? Open them? Close my *eyes*. What? All these thoughts flew through my mind in about a quarter of a second and then one voice prevailed above all others.

You've imagined this a thousand times! Don't screw it up!

So I closed my eyes and hoped for the best.

And then, the front door creaked. My eyes flew open, Jared jumped back a step, and my father cleared his throat. Loudly.

Oh God. Oh God. Oh God.

Everything inside of me deflated. One second I was feeling all warm and fuzzy with the scent of Jared's cologne enveloping me and the tingle of his lips just millimeters away. The next second I was staring into the angry eyes of my father. Major buzz kill.

"Dad! We were just—"

"You must be Jared," my father interrupted me. His stare was colder than granite.

"Nice to meet you, Mr. Grace," Jared said smoothly, offering his hand. My dad hesitated for a second, then shook it.

"It's getting late," he said, "You should probably be heading home."

"Absolutely," Jared said, putting his hands in his pockets. "Gracie, I'll call you tomorrow?" he said.

"Uh . . . sure," I told him.

"You have lessons tomorrow, Cassandra," my father said. "And you need to work out with Lola."

Could he *be* any more embarrassing? "I know," I said through my teeth. "But I'm sure I'll have time for a phone call," I assured Jared.

"Good. I had a great time tonight," Jared said, all business. There was none of the warmth or attraction in his eyes anymore. Even though I understood why, it was like a knife to the heart. "Good night, Mr. Grace."

"'Night," my father said, his voice gruff.

Jared squeezed my arm as he walked by me, and was off. The moment the door of his car slammed, all the adrenaline that had gone into getting almost-kissed redirected itself at my father. I had been on the verge of what was potentially the most romantic moment of my entire life, and he had purposely interrupted it. I whirled on him, my blood boiling. I had never been so angry.

"How could you do that to me?" I shouted.

"Cassandra—"

"Don't call me Cassandra like I'm some little five-year-old!" I yelled, storming past him into the house. "I'm eighteen, Dad. Can't I even get a little privacy around here? A little respect?"

My father closed the door and turned slowly. I could tell he was trying to hold in his temper. "Maybe I'll start treating you with respect when you start making some better choices."

"What? Are you kidding me?" I shouted, slamming my bag down on the counter that separated the kitchen from the front entryway. "I got into college. I got a scholarship. I work my butt off around here trying to earn my own money and I've never *ever* done one thing wrong. I've never gotten detention. Never rolled in here drunk or had even one cigarette. You really think I'm making bad choices?!"

My mother appeared at the end of the hallway in her nightgown, her arms wrapped around herself. She looked confused and a little scared.

Not that I could blame her. There was hardly any yelling in this house. Ever.

"Yes, I do. I know I said that you could go tonight, but I did not appreciate the casual way in which you dismissed dinner with your mother and me," he said, pressing his hand into the counter so hard his knuckles turned white. "And I don't want you hanging out with that Kent kid anymore. Or any summer locals for that matter. It never ends well."

My jaw dropped and I let out a high-pitched sound somewhere between a squeak and a scoff. "What do you mean it never ends well? I've never hung out with them before."

"And I'd prefer to keep it that way," he said. "Every time a Lake Loganer has gotten mixed up with them, there's trouble."

"Dad! I'm not just another Lake Loganer!" I shouted. "Don't you trust me at all?"

"Of course I do!" he snapped back. "It's the Kents I don't trust."

"You don't even *know* Jared!" I replied, hot tears of frustration stinging my eyes.

"Well, I know his parents," he responded.

"You are not to hang around that kid and that's final."

I took a deep breath and blinked back the torrent of tears that was threatening to overflow. I couldn't believe I was actually arguing with my father. I couldn't believe we were standing here screaming at each other in the middle of the night. But most of all I couldn't believe how unreasonable he was being. I snatched my purse off the counter and slung the strap over my shoulder.

"Well, it's really not up to you, is it?" I said stonily. "I'm not a little kid anymore, Dad. You can't tell me who I can and can't see."

My father blinked, taken aback by my tone. I knew he was about to come up with a comeback, so I turned and hustled down to my room as fast as possible. My mother called after me, but I simply slammed the door and burst into tears. I had never spoken to my father like that before. I had never seen him look that disappointed in me before.

How had the greatest night of my life just turned into the absolute worst?

* * *

Eventually I dried my eyes, changed into a tank top and cotton shorts, and crawled into bed. Suddenly I was exhausted, but I knew I wasn't going to be able to sleep. I propped my pillows up against the headboard and sat with my sheet covering my knees. I could hear my parents talking in low, but intense, tones out in the kitchen. From what I imagined I could hear, my father was seriously angry and my mother was defending me.

Finally, I heard the floorboards squeak and their bedroom door close. For a moment I thought they had both gone to bed, but then I heard my mother's footsteps coming down the hall. I held my breath. She knocked lightly and opened the door.

"Mind if I come in?" she asked, peeking her head inside.

"Sure," I said. I reached over and turned on my bedside lamp. My heart felt sick and my insides were all twisted up. I just hoped my mom was here with good news—not something that would make it all feel worse.

She sat down on the end of my mattress

and rubbed my foot through the sheet.

"Cassie, about what your father said earlier," she began. "He just doesn't want to see you get hurt. We know you're getting older, but it's kind of hard for us to stop wanting to protect you."

"I don't get it, Mom," I said, pulling my knees up and hugging them to me. "What is the big deal with the Kents? So Jared's mom fell in love and left town. Big deal! That shouldn't make them public enemy number one."

My mother took a deep breath. "The story is not that simple."

I tipped my head back in frustration. I was so sick of cryptic answers. Of gossipy stories and muddled facts. "So tell me the story!" I said. "Come on, Mom. If you guys want me to understand, then just tell me. I'm a big girl. I can take it."

My mom looked at me in the semidarkness, then turned and lifted her legs up onto the bed. She sat there Indian-style in her nightgown, and folded the end of my quilt over her own knees.

"Okay, Cassie. I don't like to talk about this because I don't like dredging up bad memories, but now that the Kents have come back into our lives, I suppose you should know," she said.

I leaned back, still holding on to my knees, and settled in. Half the kids in my high school would have killed to be there at that moment, getting the real Kent saga from a woman who had actually been there. But all I cared about at that moment was how it might affect me and Jared.

"Robert Kent was this gorgeous teenage hot shot who came up here every summer with his parents and his two older brothers," my mother began. "The brothers were totally suave and obnoxious, but mostly kept to themselves like most invaders, so they were no big deal. Robert, however, was another story. He would get up here before Lake Logan High was even done for the year and he'd hang out in the parking lot with his Corvette, talking to local girls, taking them out for drives. Every girl who met him completely fell in love with him. Except me, of course. I was already taken."

I smiled at this, recalling the picture of my parents in their senior yearbook: "Class Couple." So cheesy, but so ridiculously cute.

"Anyway, as you know, Susan Morris was

my best friend, but as adventurous as she was around here, she was totally shy when it came to boys. Plus she wasn't the fashion-plate type. She was pretty, but not into clothes and makeup and all that. Robert tried to talk to her once and she basically turned red and ran away," my mom continued. "After that, he didn't bother with her, but for two years, Robert was all she could talk about. She daydreamed about him. Wrote his name all over her books. And even though he came up here every summer and broke some other girl's heart, she never stopped thinking that if she could just get up the guts to talk to him, they would fall madly in love."

I knew the type. Those girls who just wanted to tame a player. Somehow it never seemed to work out like they planned.

"So then senior year rolls around and suddenly Susan starts to experiment with makeup and starts reading fashion magazines," my mom said with a sigh. "We all thought it was great. You know how girls are. We'd been telling Sue to fix herself up for years. She was the smartest girl in our class and she got into all the Ivy League schools. I figured she just wanted a new look for college or whatever. But then, that summer, Robert shows up and Susan tells me she's going to go talk to him. I said, 'Yeah, right.' There was no way the Sue I knew had the guts to do that. But she did. Right there at Pete's in front of all these Lake Loganers and everyone. Robert took one look at her and that was it. We all knew there was going to be trouble."

"So for the next four weeks, Susan and Robert spent all their time together. They ran around town like they owned it, racing his car, stealing flowers from one of the roadside stands, just generally acting like morons," my mother said. "At first Susan and I still hung out, but she changed pretty quickly. She had no interest in going to the lake anymore or going horse-back riding. It was all about Robert's friends and the country club and day trips to the city. One time I didn't see her for a week, so I called the Kents' to try to talk to her and Robert picked up the phone. He told me Susan didn't need farm trash friends anymore and to stop stalking her." My mother looked down at the quilt and picked at a loose string. "I wouldn't have believed him, but I could hear her laughing in the background. I hung up the phone and that was the last time I ever heard her voice. Laughing at me."

My heart panged and I felt sick to my stomach. I couldn't imagine what I would do if Donna dropped me that way. If she laughed while someone insulted me. I'd probably crawl under the covers and cry for days.

"He completely changed her. She just took off with him halfway through the summer and sent her parents a postcard saying they had eloped. After that they never heard from her again. Didn't even bother telling me she was married. She had enrolled at Harvard, but she never went," my mom continued. "Her dad had a heart attack a few years later and passed. Then her mom died a couple years after that. Supposedly she took care of their funerals, but I never saw her. The Susan I knew never would have ignored her education or dropped her family like that. It was just totally awful."

I swallowed back a lump that had formed in my throat. I wondered if Jared knew even half of what I had just heard.

"I'm so sorry, Mom," I said. "I had no idea."

"Well, your dad went through all that with me," my mother said. "So you can imagine why he's a little wary of the Kents. Susan broke my heart and I guess he just doesn't want to see Jared break yours."

"But he won't, Mom," I said, straightening my legs and leaning forward. "I really like him, but it's not like I'm going to run off with him and get married. I mean, seriously. This is me. Reliable, predictable Cassie. Are you really worried about that?"

My mom looked at me, then cracked a smile. "No. I suppose not."

"So, can you talk to Dad?" I asked. "I don't want him to hate Jared. This summer could be really, *really* horrible if he does."

Taking a deep breath, my mom reached out and ran her hand down the side of my face, briefly cupping my chin between her finger and thumb.

"I'll see what I can do," she said with a small smile.

I grabbed her into a hug and squeezed my eyes shut. "Thanks, Mom."

She rubbed my back, then broke away and

stood up. "Good night, hon," she said. "Sleep well."

"I will," I said. "Mom?"

She paused on her way out of the room. "Yeah, Cass?"

"Do you think you'll see her? Susan, I mean. Now that she's back in town?"

My mother paused, her hand on the doorknob, and smiled sadly at me. "I don't think so. I don't really feel the need to go down that road again."

I felt my chest well up with sorrow for her, but I suppose I understood. I can't imagine ever wanting to speak to Donna again if she did something like that to me. Maybe if she had made some kind of effort over the years, but the fact that Susan had never even tried to make it up to my mom just made the whole thing that much more horrible.

"See you in the morning," my mom said.

"See ya."

Then she closed the door and left me to stare at the ceiling, a million different thoughts of hope, betrayal, and sadness swirling around in my mind.

Chapter Eleven

"Jared Kent. Your first kiss was almost with Jared Kent?" Donna squealed, nearly dropping her ice cream cone.

The Hendersons were sitting at the next picnic table over, trying to keep their kids from dripping sprinkles all over themselves, but they were still interested enough to glance over at us. In fact, half the crowd outside the Dairy Go Round fell suspiciously quiet. The last thing I needed was the entire town talking about this, asking my mom and dad about it, starting a whole new rumor about how I was going to be the next Susan Morris.

"The key word being 'almost,'" I said. "And shhhh."

I shoved a spoonful of my chocolate ice

cream into my mouth and stared at Corey Henderson until she turned away. The girl may have had two kids already, but she was only four years older than me. I figure that still gave me the right to stare her down when she was eavesdropping. It's not like she was my *elder* or something.

"I'm sorry, I just can't believe it," Donna said, tucking a wayward curl behind her ear. "My best friend and *the* Jared Kent."

Her green eyes were bright with excitement. For a girl who was initially opposed to me even *talking* to Jared, she seemed a little stoked over this news. I had even been reluctant to tell her, thinking she was going to slap me upside the head. Instead she looked as if I had just given her the inside scoop on the latest Hollywood über-couple.

"I thought you and Derek didn't want me to get mixed up with him and his crowd," I said. I mushed my ice cream around with my plastic spoon, watching as the chocolate sprinkles started to drown.

"Well, that was before I knew you really liked him. And if you like him, I like him,"

Donna said with a shrug. "Besides, how bad could he be? I mean, yeah, he was rude that first day, but I *was* slamming his mother. And anyway, he's practically famous. That always wins you points."

That was Donna Logic for you.

"Not with my dad," I mumbled.

"Forget your dad! This is your life! This is potentially your first big romance!" Donna exclaimed, growing loud again. "Defy your father! Sneak out if you have to! I don't care!"

"Uh . . . Donna?" I said, eyeing the curious/disturbed glances of the families around us.

"I'm sorry! I need someone to live vicariously through!" Donna said with a laugh. "Just don't forget your real friends while you're off planning your wedding in the Hamptons with *InStyle*."

"Donna! I am absolutely, positively *not* getting married," I said. "I haven't even been kissed yet."

I saw a couple of kids from school lean over their table and whisper as they watched us. My face burned. Maybe dating Jared really *would* be like being famous. All we needed now was some paparazzi and we'd be good to go.

"Can we maybe change the subject?" I asked.

"Okay, fine," Donna said, crunching into her cone. "You have off on Friday, right?"

"Thank God," I said with a sigh. "Twenty-four hours with no whining, screaming, crying, or mud-throwing."

"Well, I was thinking . . . it's that time of year!" Donna said brightly.

Instantly, my spirits lifted. "Yeah it is," I cheered.

"Outlet run!" we both called out, high-fiving over the table.

Corey's husband let out a huff and made a big show of moving to the other end of his table, away from us. Clearly he thought we were being obnoxiously loud. But come on! What kind of world do we live in when a couple of girls can't cheer over their annual shopping trip?

"I will pick you up at ten A.M. sharp," Donna told me.

"So . . . ten thirty, then?" I teased. Donna had never once been on time since I had known her. And I'd known her my entire life.

"Ha ha," she said flatly. "It shouldn't be too bad since it's not a weekend, but we still want to get there semi-early to beat the crowds."

"I know the drill," I told her. "I'll be ready. Is Derek coming this year?" I asked, raising one eyebrow.

Donna and I had been making this trip together every summer since we were in middle school (back then our moms would take us). Last year, for the first time, we had made the mistake of inviting Derek along. He had made us miserable all day, whining about how his feet hurt and how everything was still expensive, even though the stores were supposed to be outlets.

"Please. I think we learned our lesson, no?" Donna said. "My brother is to shopping what ants are to a picnic."

I laughed. "How long have you been sitting on that one?"

"Oh, about a year," Donna replied with a sly smile. "You have the cash, right?" she asked. "You're not gonna, like, bogart the wardrobe money for Lola's entry fee."

"Are you kidding? My mom gives me a

little money for this trip every year and it is earmarked for this specific purpose," I said. "I am *not* going to college next year in the same old crappy jeans."

Donna grinned and popped the last bit of her ice cream cone into her mouth. "That's my girl."

As always, I was ready to go early on Friday morning. Donna was notoriously late, me notoriously early. Even when I *tried* to be late —fashionably or otherwise —I was always the first one to arrive wherever we were going. Part of my reliability, I guess. So there I was, money in my purse, hair in a French braid so I wouldn't have to keep brushing it out every time I pulled something over my head, wondering how late, exactly, Donna would be. I was hanging out in the kitchen flipping through the morning paper when I heard the now-familiar sound of Jared's BMW pulling into the driveway.

I jumped right out of my chair, glad that my dad was out for the day. We had spoken since the Jared fight, but not much and definitely not about Jared himself. Whenever Jared called —

which was almost every night—I took the phone back to my room and kept my voice down. We gabbed for hours about school—he had gone to some chic private academy and was headed to Columbia in the fall—our friends, movies, books, and a million other things. And the whole time I would be whispering by my window, hoping my father wouldn't burst in and make me hang up the phone. I had never talked on the phone with a guy so much in my life—except *maybe* Derek. The last thing I wanted was for all the excitement to be ruined by my dad flipping out.

I had no idea whether my mother had talked to my father as she had promised, and if so, whether the conversation had been successful. To be honest, I was kind of afraid to ask. If no one brought it up again, maybe we could pretend like it had never happened.

Jared and I met out on the front walk. Down in the paddock, Penny Haberman, one of the stable hands and riding instructors, led Marci Crewson through a series of low jumps on her horse, Coco.

"What are you doing here?" I asked Jared.

"Good morning to you, too," he replied teasingly.

I laughed. "Sorry. I just never would have pegged you for a morning person."

"I'm not, usually," he said. Twirling his keys around his finger, he looked around at the view of the hills—the wispy clouds chasing each other across a clear blue sky. "I don't know. I think this place is having some kind of effect on me."

You could have knocked me over with a finger-flick. Was Jared Kent actually admitting that he was starting to like Lake Logan?

"So I was thinking, a girl such as you should not go through life without knowing how to drive stick," he said. "So I've come to offer my services," he said, adding a comical bow. "My expertise is yours."

Huh. A girl such as me? What did that mean, exactly? I was very tempted to go with him and see if I could find out.

"That is, if you're not busy earning that entry fee of yours," he added.

By now Jared was entirely familiar with my plans for county competition domination.

Every night he grilled me about Lola and what the jumps were like and how many prizes I had won. He seemed very interested in the whole process, which was very cool.

"No, no lessons today. But I do have plans," I told him, somewhat reluctantly. "Donna's picking me up. We're going shopping."

Jared smirked. "Where? Wonder Mart?"

I had to laugh. "No. We're going to the outlets."

"Ah, yes. The outlets," Jared said. "My mother's already been there about five times. You can take the girl out of Manhattan, but you can't take the shopper out of the girl. Well, another time, then," he said, turning away.

"Wait," I blurted.

Wait? What was I doing? Was it really *that* impossible for me to let him walk off? Maybe it was the fresh morning air or the fact that he had rolled out of bed and come right over to see a "girl such as me," but I didn't want him to leave. He eyed me quizzically.

"Hang on a sec," I said.

I jogged back inside and grabbed the phone, hitting speed dial for the Policastro house. Derek picked up on the first ring.

"Whaddup, Cassie?" he said.

"Hey. Lemme ask you something," I said, biting my lip. "How late, exactly, is Donna running?"

"Is she supposed to be meeting you somewhere?" he said with a groan. "I'd better get her up. Donna!" he shouted, holding the phone away. "Donna, you freak! Get out of bed!"

"Wait, wait, wait!" I said with a laugh.

"What?" Derek asked, returning.

"Just . . . tell her she can take her time," I said, smiling.

"Will do," he replied. "What are you guys doing, anyway? Why wasn't I invited?"

"I could tell you, but then I'd have to kill you," I said. "Catch ya later."

I hung up the phone before he could ask me anything else and practically skipped out the door. Jared was waiting patiently, watching Penny and Marci.

"Okay, let's go," I said.

His entire face lit up as he turned around. "Sweet."

"But we can't be long," I told him, my pulse

skipping around like it always did when I was with him. "It'll have to be a quick lesson."

"We'll need an open space. Like a parking lot or something," Jared said.

I considered this as I opened the passenger side door to his sleek auto. "I have the perfect place."

I held my breath as I toured the BMW around the concrete island in the center of the Logan Lanes parking lot. Or what had once been the Logan Lanes. The bowling alley had closed its doors four years ago and the roof had collapsed during a blizzard this past winter. Weeds pushed up through cracks in the asphalt parking lot and the far end had become a dumping ground for rusted-out cars, old tires, an ancient refrigerator, and various other oversized garbage items. It was an eyesore, but a great deserted spot for a driving lesson.

"Good. See? You're getting it," Jared said, draping his arm over the back of my seat.

I was already sweating from concentrating and driving under the rising sun, but the touch of his arm on the back of my neck doubled my body temperature.

Concentrate, Cass, I told myself. *Do not drive his car into a wall.*

For the first half hour, all I had done was buck around and stall out. Now, for the first time, I had gone from first gear to second and from second to third with almost no stuttering.

"Now try slowing down," Jared said.

I eased up on the gas, put the clutch to the floor and downshifted into second. It took a moment for me to find the gear and we coasted, but then I found it and we lurched once as we slowed down.

"Oops. Sorry," I said.

"No. It's good," Jared said. "Another half hour of this and you'll be an old pro."

I glanced at the clock on the dashboard and shoved my foot down on the brake and clutch at the same time. Jared flew forward, got caught by his seat belt, and bounced back.

"You definitely know how to stop," he said, rubbing his chest where the belt had squeezed him.

"Is that the right time?" I asked, my throat going dry.

Jared checked his chunky watch. "Yeah. It's eleven fifteen. Why?"

Omigod. Donna. She was going to *kill* me. She looked forward to this trip all year and here I was, more than an hour late.

"I told you this had to be a short lesson!" I wailed, throwing the car into first gear and then second, heading for the exit.

"You were the one who kept saying 'ten more minutes,'" Jared said. "Who knew you were such a perfectionist?"

Oh, God. He was right. This was all my fault. Between enjoying my time with him and loving the whole stick-shift thing, I had subconsciously blocked out the fact that I was supposed to be hanging out with Donna.

I paused at the edge of the parking lot, then pulled out onto Jones Road. Jared glanced at me out of the corner of his eye. He looked a little skittish.

"What?" I said, accelerating.

"You're driving home?" he asked. "Out here on the actual road?"

My heart hit my throat and for a second I was practically sick with fear. What was I doing?

I didn't know how to drive this thing! I gripped the wheel with one hand, the ball on top of the stick shift with the other. Okay, it was just the quiet streets of Lake Logan. I could not let Jared see me panic over something this simple.

"Yeah," I said with some effort. "You're Mr. I-Love-Danger, right? Well, hold on."

Jared studied me for a second, then laughed and leaned back in his seat. "I think I'm a good influence on you, Gracie."

I grinned at the compliment, but the irony of the statement wasn't lost on me. Yeah, he had taught me to drive stick and I was, at that very moment, taking a bit of a risk. But my best friend was also sitting back at my house wondering where the hell I was. So was that a good influence, or a bad influence?

Maybe she hasn't been there that long, I thought as I turned onto Town Line Road. After all, she hadn't even been up when I had called at nine thirty. Maybe she had taken her time getting ready and had only arrived fifteen minutes ago. Yeah. That was a definite possibility. She probably wouldn't even be mad.

"Wow. You're a natural," Jared said as I

downshifted and turned into the driveway at the ranch. I didn't signal, but I also didn't buck as I reaccelerated. A girl could only concentrate on so many things at once.

"Thanks," I told him, pleased.

My smile disappeared, however, the second I saw Donna standing outside my house, her arms crossed over her chest. I watched her jaw drop as she glimpsed me behind the wheel of the Beemer. I parked next to Donna's beat-up old Jetta and killed the engine, my heart pounding.

"Nice work!" Jared said.

I was about to respond when Donna strode around the front of the garage. She paused in front of the car and made a big show of checking her watch.

"Donna, I am so sorry," I said, getting out of the car.

"Where the heck have you been?" she asked. "I've been waiting here for over half an hour."

"Jared showed up to teach me how to drive stick and I guess I lost track of time," I explained.

"Hi," Jared said uncertainly.

Donna just shot him a withering look. "So, what? You can't even call me?" she asked.

"Donna, I know I'm late, but come on. It's not that big a deal," I said. "You're *always* late."

Donna balked. "Yeah, but that's part of my charm."

Jared laughed. "That's funny. I like her," he said to me.

"I don't remember asking for your approval," Donna said flatly, narrowing her eyes at him.

Whoa. Where had *that* come from? The other day she had been all psyched about me dating Jared and now she was biting his head off. Was my best friend going schizo on me? Jared raised his hands in surrender and clamped his mouth shut. Wise move.

"Look, I said I was sorry," I told her patiently. "Can't we just go now?"

"I don't really think I'm in the mood anymore," Donna said, pulling her keys out of her purse. She yanked open the door to the Jetta with a creak and flopped down onto the seat.

"Donna," I said.

"I'll call you later," she told me.

Then she peeled out of there so quickly I had to jump back to keep from having my feet flattened.

"Wow. Two for two with Donna," Jared said, finally climbing out of the car. "Girl's kind of got a temper, huh?"

I sighed and hugged myself. "She does love her drama," I said, my heart turning. I had expected Donna to be irritated, but not *so* irritated that she would call off our shopping trip. "I don't get it. We look forward to this trip every year. I can't believe she doesn't still want to go."

"It's me. I have this effect on girls," Jared said matter-of-factly, leaning back against his car and putting his hands in the pockets of his shorts. "They either love me or they hate me."

"I don't think she *hates* you," I replied. *Yesterday she was all ready to pick out her bridesmaid dress for our Hamptons wedding,* I added silently.

"Are you kidding? Did you see the way she just looked at me?" he asked.

I laughed. "Well, okay. Maybe she hates you *right now.* Like I said, she's dramatic."

Jared stood up straight and clapped his hands together. "Well, we're going to have to do something about this."

"Like what?" I asked.

"Oh, I have a plan," he said in a self-satisfied

way. "You just get Donna and meet me at the lake tomorrow morning. Bright and early. Eight o'clock."

"I can't," I said. "I have lessons tomorrow morning." Not that I *wanted* to be there. It was Josh and Seth Locke again. Little monsters. Followed by a new student, Olivia Watson—another child invader.

"Can't you get someone to cover them?" Jared asked. "This is important."

"Why is it so important?" I asked him.

"Because, I can't have your best friend hating me all summer!" Jared said, as if it was the most obvious thing in the world. "That could really put a cramp in . . . you know . . . everything." And then he blushed. He actually averted his gaze and blushed. Jared Kent.

I smiled slowly, unable to believe that I, Cassie Grace, had inspired Jared Kent to get all awkward and tongue-tied and flushed. There was going to be an "everything" this summer? How cool was that?

"Okay," I said. "I'll see what I can do."

Chapter Twelve

Penny was sweeping out the stable office when I caught her later that afternoon. Her choppy red hair was plastered with sweat to the back of her neck and she had taken off her long-sleeved shirt and tied it around her waist, exposing her tight tank top and totally ripped arms. When Penny wasn't working at the ranch, she was boxing at the gym in Morganville. Dino Anderson claimed he had once seen her fight in an actual ring and knock the other girl out in three rounds, but it was a claim that had never been substantiated. I had never asked Penny about it myself. She wasn't much for talking about herself.

"Hey, Penny. Can I ask you a favor?" I said.

Lola moseyed over to the gate at the sound

of my voice and nuzzled my shoulder. I petted her snout in response. She was probably irritated that I hadn't taken her out yet today, but because of the day off and the shopping trip I had foregone my morning ride. *So* not worth it, obviously. I would have to make it up to Lola with an evening stroll.

Penny kept sweeping. "What's up, kid?"

"I was wondering if you could maybe cover my lessons tomorrow morning," I said. "You can have the fees, obviously."

She straightened up and fixed me with a steely-eyed stare.

"What?" I said, taken aback.

"Nothing." She grabbed my wrist, holding it between her thumb and forefinger. "Pulse seems normal." She took off her glove and felt my forehead. "Not hot. So we can rule out delusional fever. What happened? Hell freeze over?"

I cracked a smile. "I know it's not like me—"

"Not like you?" she said, returning to the broom. "All you've been talking about all year is making money for that entry fee. Now two weeks into the summer you're giving up your lessons? What gives?"

She was right, of course. The last thing I should be doing was passing off my clients. Especially three of them. But how was I supposed to turn down Jared's invitation and thwart his attempt to apologize to Donna? It was so sweet that he even wanted to try. Plus, if everything worked out, there would be the added bonus of my best friend and the guy I *really* wanted to kiss getting along. That would definitely be a plus.

But I had a feeling that Penny wouldn't understand any of this. That she would, in fact, whack me with that broom handle for suggesting I choose fun over work. So I decided to keep it simple.

"I just have something really important to do," I said. "Please. I promise I won't ask again. It's just this one time."

She paused in her sweeping and leaned on the broom. "How many students you got?"

"The Locke boys come at ten o'clock and this new girl Olivia is coming at eleven thirty," I said hopefully. "I'll be honest, the Locke kids are no angels, and I haven't met Olivia yet. You could be in for it."

Penny smiled and scoffed, shaking her head. "You really know how to sell a girl."

I felt a rush of panic. "No! They're not that bad," I lied. "Please, Penny? I just—"

"I was being sarcastic, kid," she said, cutting me off. "You know I like a challenge. And I definitely like some extra cash."

"Really?" I squealed, causing Miss Piggy to whinny in irritation in the next stall. "Thank you so much!"

"And this is okay with your parents, right?" she said, raising her eyebrows at me.

I turned away, shoved my hand into the open bag of oats on the floor, and crossed my fingers. "Yeah," I said. "They don't mind."

"All right then. I'm in," Penny said.

I brought out a handful of oats and held them under Lola's snout. As she munched away and licked at my palm, I tried not to feel too guilty about lying. After all, if anyone got in trouble for this, it would be me, not Penny. I just had to remember that it was for a good cause. Besides, a girl had to live a *little* during her last summer before college . . . right?

Now I just had one more person to convince.

* * *

Donna was dumping freshly popped popcorn from the kettle into the warmer when I walked through the doors of the theater and into the deserted lobby. The seven thirty show had already started and the nine forty-five was far off. The place was silent as a tomb.

"Hey," I said.

The kettle fell back with a clang and Donna turned around, hand to heart.

"First you dis me, then you try to kill me?" she said. I'd love to say that she was joking, but her voice had no smile in it.

"Still mad, huh?" I said. I walked over and rested my arms on the glass countertop above the candy case.

"I just wiped that down," Donna said flatly.

I pulled my arms away. She was really not giving me an inch.

"Donna, what's wrong?" I asked her, swallowing against a lump in my throat. "Is it just that I was late or is there something else going on here?"

Donna took a deep breath and leaned back against the counter behind her. She crossed her arms over her chest and studied me, as if she were trying to gauge whether or not to say anything. For a moment I actually felt uncomfortable. Since when was there anything Donna couldn't say to me?

Finally she sighed and dropped her arms. "Look. It's just . . . this is our last summer," she said. "And if you go and get a boyfriend on me and start making plans without me and forgetting about me and stuff, I may just have to kill myself."

I felt as if the worn carpet had dropped out from underneath me. "Donna! I would *never* forget about you." Even though I kind of had that morning. But that was more about my obsession with mastering the stick shift than Jared. Kind of. "Besides, he's not even my boyfriend. We're just . . . hanging out."

"Great. So he's not even your boyfriend and already you're dissing me for him," she said. "This does not bode well."

"I don't get it," I told her. "I thought you were happy about me and Jared."

"I was. I mean, I am!" Donna said, growing frustrated. "I just don't want to lose you, all right? It's our last summer before college." She looked down and picked at the bottom hem of her maroon jacket. "I just . . . I don't want to get left behind."

Tears filled her voice and instantly caused my eyes to well up. It *killed* me that I had made Donna sound like that. I would love to blame it on Donna's drama again, but we had both been like this for weeks. Ever since we'd realized that high school was, in fact, going to come to an end, we had been noting several lasts with overdone fondness. Our last cafeteria French fries. Our last climb up the rope in gym class. The last time we'd see a freshman trip up the steps outside the auditorium. This last summer thing was about fifty times bigger than all of that combined.

"Donna, I am not going to leave you behind, all right? No matter what," I told her firmly. "In fact, Jared invited us to hang out at the lake with him tomorrow. *Both* of us. He feels bad about what happened and he wants you guys to be friends."

Donna looked up, half smiling. "I don't want to be a third wheel. . . ."

"Please," I said to her, tucking my chin. "You

and I are the wheels. If anyone's a third, it's the invader."

That brought out the true grin and Donna reached over the counter to hug me. The edge of the glass case pressed painfully into my chest, but I didn't care. At that moment, all that mattered was that everything was okay between me and Donna.

The next morning I was up at the crack of dawn, as always, doing the morning chores with my father. We worked in silence, the air between us still cold. Afterward, I took Lola out for a morning ride, encroaching on the Kent property as always. Whenever I went up there now I half hoped I would bump into Jared again, both so I could see him and so I could show him that his grandstand about trespassing hadn't scared me away, but so far the ATV seemed to be taking a rest.

Lola and I got a good workout, and when we got back, I showered quickly, threw on my bathing suit under my clothes, and waited in my room for my mom to get into the shower. My heart pounded with fear and self-loathing as I crept out the side door and closed it quietly. I couldn't believe I was sneaking out of my house. That I hadn't even told my parents I had dumped my morning lessons on Penny. As much as I tried to convince myself that it would all be fine, I knew otherwise. My parents did not appreciate people who shirked responsibility. They were going to go nuts when they found out. But there was no turning back now.

Dad was in the stables with a couple of contractors when I grabbed my dirt bike and sped out of there to meet my friends at the lake, hopefully unseen. The moment I had turned onto Town Line Road and was free and clear of the ranch, my nervousness was replaced with exhilaration. I was free. I had gotten away with it. I was going to spend the morning with Donna and Jared and not with the loony Locke boys.

I sat back in the seat and relished the feeling of the wind in my hair. For once, I was going to forget about being responsible and just have a good time. I could deal with the consequences later.

Chapter Thirteen

"*It* is *way* too early in the morning for this," Donna said, adding a huge yawn. She was wearing her American flag bikini, denim shorts, and big tortoiseshell sunglasses and sucking coffee from a Dunkin' Donuts travel mug. "Don't tell me Jared's a morning person. You know how I hate morning people."

"*I'm* a morning person," I reminded her. "I've been up for more than three hours already."

"Yeah, and you are way too perky," she grumbled. "Why are we friends again?"

"Very funny," I replied.

I leaned back on my elbows on the beach blanket and tipped my face toward the strengthening sun. This early in the morning the beach was empty except for me, Donna, and a couple of ducks paddling around near the shore. Out on the lake, a couple of fishing boats were anchored and I could see the poles sticking up into the air, though I couldn't make out who the fishermen were. So far no one had caught anything, but I knew these guys could stay out there for hours, just soaking in the sun and the peacefulness. Even farther out, a large sailboat cut slowly across the lake, probably heading for the invader-heavy sailing club on the eastern shore. A light breeze ruffled the leaves on the trees and I let out a luxuriant sigh. These were the moments I appreciated Lake Logan's laziness. This was the life.

"So, what are we doing here again?" Donna asked me.

"I don't know. Jared said he had some kind of plan."

Personally, I thought it was just cool that Jared was so gung ho to make up yesterday's slight to Donna. Clearly he didn't take after his old man—the guy who had told off my mother over the phone while *her* best friend laughed in the background.

Huh. Maybe apples fall farther from the tree

than most people would have you believe. Maybe I'd have to tell the folks about this later.

"Um . . . what's that noise?" Donna asked, pushing her sunglasses up onto her head. I sat up, just now noticing the insistent buzzing sound. "Chainsaw?" I said.

"Nah. Too high-pitched," Donna said. She put her coffee cup down in the sand and pushed herself up. "Besides, I think it's coming from the lake."

I stood up as the buzzing grew louder and louder. A whoop and a shout echoed over the water and suddenly a pair of jet skis sped into view, spewing water everywhere as they cut haphazard wakes through the shallow part of the lake. I recognized Jared instantly, as he cut right over his partner's wake, executing a little jump. The jet ski slapped back down on the surface of the lake only a few yards from one of the fishing boats. I closed my eyes against the shouts of anger and tried not to smile.

This type of hot-dogging wasn't illegal, but was definitely frowned upon this close to the shore. Even out deep, speedboats and jet skis were few and far between. We were all about tranquility in Lake Logan and most people hated it when that tranquility was tampered with. Especially if the tampering was being done by hot-shot invaders.

"What the hell do they think they're doing?" Donna blurted. She sounded indignant, but when I turned to look at her, she was grinning, too.

How could you not? Jared and his friend were speeding toward the shore now, all wet and grinning and being boys. That kind of thing had an effect on girls like us. All girls, actually.

The boys drove their jet skis right up onto the sand, creating deep ruts in the beach. Jared's friend was tall and broad like a football player with curly blond hair that he shook out like a Golden Retriever, spraying water all around. He had a boyish smile and freckles across his nose and as he loped over to us, I couldn't help thinking he would make a great Tom Sawyer.

"Sweet ride, man," he said, holding out his hand to Jared.

They slapped palms and caught their breath as they joined us near the beach blanket. It took all my self-control not to stare at Jared's glistening bare chest.

"Ladies," Jared said with a smile. "I'd like you to meet my best friend, Christopher. Chris, this is Donna and Cassie."

"How's it going?" Chris said, lifting his chin. "Which one's yours?" he asked Jared.

I turned purple and Jared rolled his eyes. "Nice one, man. Very charming."

"I'm just kidding!" Christopher said with a laugh.

Donna laughed as well. I could tell by the look on her face that she was already imagining what their children might look like. Christopher was exactly Donna's type. She had been fostering a crush on Mike Grossman as long as I could remember, but had never gotten up the guts to do anything about it. Once again I was left wondering how Jared was able to read people so well. Could he tell what Donna's type was just by looking at her?

"So, you just made a few enemies out there, you know," I said lightly.

"Those old guys? Please. They need a little excitement in their lives," Christopher said. "Gets the blood flowing."

"You guys want to go for a ride?" Jared asked. "They're built for two."

"Absolutely," Donna said, already halfway down the beach. Christopher smiled over his shoulder at Jared, clearly liking what he saw, and followed her.

Jared pressed his fist into his hand and brought his hands to his chin, watching them. The action made his biceps flex in a totally distracting way. "Well, what do you think?" he asked.

"I think you may be a genius," I told him.

"If you saw my grades, you'd take that back," he said with a half smile. "Come on, Gracie. Let's go have some fun."

The boys took off, at a much more respectable speed, and cut across the lake to the west. I tried not to think about the fact that I had my arms wrapped around a half-naked Jared with my chest pressing into his back. Instead, I concentrated on the water ahead, hoping he wouldn't cut too close to the fishermen again and cause more problems. I was surprised when I realized we were headed for the far northwest shore, where most locals had trekked at one time or another for a little one-on-one time with their significant others. (Not me, of course.) Most invaders didn't even know this small stretch of beach existed, which was why the Lake Loganers preferred it for private moments. Apparently, Jared and his friend had done their research.

As we approached the shore, I noticed there was something on the beach, but I couldn't tell what it was until we were right on top of it. Laid out on the center of the sand was a large red blanket, a real picnic basket, a big Thermos, and Tupperware tubs filled with food.

"What did you guys do?" I said, placing my chin on Jared's shoulder as he parked the jet ski on the sand.

"You like it?" Jared asked, turning his face so quickly our lips almost touched.

I slid back, embarrassed by his closeness, and lifted my leg over the jet ski. "Definitely."

Christopher and Donna were already prying open the Tupperware, and I could see that the guys had brought a gorgeous fruit salad, several muffins, scrambled eggs, and slices of cooked bacon.

"Omigosh, this smells *so* good," Donna said. Apparently, the boy and the jet ski ride had knocked the grogginess right out of her. "How did you get all this out here?"

"Chris and I made an extra trip this morning," Jared said, sitting down on the edge of the blanket. "There's a camping grill in there if you want to heat anything up," he added, pointing at a green metal box next to the picnic basket.

"Wow, I'm impressed," Donna said.

"Well, we're impressive," Christopher joked, sitting down so close to her their thighs touched.

Donna blushed. Her curly hair had turned into a wild mane on the ride and she smoothed it back into a low ponytail. She looked beautiful, all flushed and happy and wet.

"I'm growing on you now, aren't I?" Jared asked Donna in a mock-cocky way.

"Like a weed," Donna shot back.

As we all gathered around and dug in, my heart felt as light as air. Suddenly, everything was falling into place. My conscience tried to remind me that at that very moment, my father was probably reading the note I had left him and freaking out, but I chose to ignore that fact. I was going to have fun if it killed me.

An hour later, completely stuffed and content, I got up and headed down to the water's edge to cool my feet. Jared finished putting away the mostly empty containers and joined me.

"You guys want to go for a hike and explore around here?" Christopher suggested.

"I'm in," Donna said, taking the hand Christopher offered to hoist herself up. "I need to walk off some of this food."

"You guys go ahead," I said, stretching my arms up. "I think I might take a swim."

"Me, too," Jared replied.

I turned my face away from him to hide my smile, excited that he was choosing to stay behind.

"Don't do anything I wouldn't do!" Donna trilled.

I was so mortified I could have burned to a crisp right there. "Back at ya!" I called. But they were already making their way up the path and into the trees. We could hear them laughing as they disappeared into the thick of the woods.

"I think I made it up to her," Jared said with a smile.

"You have no idea," I replied, crossing my arms over my stomach.

I took a deep breath and looked out across the lake, trying to ignore the insistent pounding of my heart. Jared was standing so close to me I could feel his warmth. But I didn't want to get all worked up if nothing was going to happen. It wasn't as if just being left alone meant we were going to suddenly start making out or something. We were standing under the sun in the middle of the day. Not the most romantic setting in the world.

Of course, it felt romantic to me.

"You know, I think I'm really starting to like this place," Jared said.

He reached up and ran the back of his finger down the side of my bare arm. That simple gesture sent so many shockwaves through my body I thought I was going to crumble.

"Yeah?" I said, turning my face toward him. Single syllables were about all I could manage at that moment.

"Yeah," he replied.

Then, before I could even close my eyes, he leaned forward and pressed his lips to mine. I was so surprised I couldn't even move. My heart raced and suddenly my brain flipped into overdrive, wanting to remember every sensation of this moment. His lips were softer than I had ever imagined. Both of his hands cupped my face and he was shaking. Was he cold, or just as nervous as I was?

When he finally pulled away, I looked into his searching eyes and grinned like an idiot. My first kiss. That was my first kiss. About a second after this fact registered, I wanted more. I reached out, grabbed Jared around the waist and pulled him toward me. I had a split second to see his flash of surprised smile before I closed my eyes and kissed him right back.

Chapter Fourteen

I practically skipped up the front walk to my house that afternoon, sun-drenched and water-logged, my lips still buzzing from a killer good-bye kiss. It was so crazy. When I woke up that morning, I had never been kissed. Now I'd been kissed *a lot*. The entire time Donna and Christopher had been gone—which was about half an hour—Jared and I did nothing but splash around in the lake, laughing, hugging and kissing. I paused and touched my fingertips to my lips, giddy. I was practically an old pro now.

Jared, Donna, Christopher, and I had spent another couple of hours swimming and loung-ing around and then Jared had driven me home in his BMW with the top down. It had been the absolute perfect day. I wasn't even thinking about that morning's missed lessons or whether or not my parents were upset. Wasn't thinking about it, at least, until I heard my father's crazed shouts coming through the window.

"I can't believe this is happening!" he yelled, slamming a kitchen cabinet so hard the window pane shook. "Who the hell do these Kents think they are?"

I glanced over my shoulder as Jared's car pulled out onto Town Line Road, leaving a cloud of dust in its wake. I wondered exactly how far Lola and I could get before either my parents or the police caught up with us. A life on the lam couldn't be *that* bad, could it?

"Thomas, calm down," my mother said. "You're going to burst a blood vessel if you keep this up."

"I don't care!" my dad shouted. Another slam, though this one sounded like he had punched a countertop. "Maybe if Robert Kent finds out he was responsible for my untimely death, he'll think twice about what he's doing."

I gulped for air. Wait a minute. *Robert* Kent?

Curiosity got the better of my paralyzing fear and I opened the screen door, letting out its telltale creak. My father fell silent and when I stepped into the kitchen doorway, they both stared at me. Dad's face was bright red from anger and exertion and my mom just looked tired.

"And where the hell have you been?" my father asked me.

"I was hanging out with Donna," I said tremulously. "What's going on?"

"Hanging out with Donna? You missed three lessons to hang out with Donna?" my father said flatly. "You tell her what's going on, Terry," he said, turning away from me. "I don't even know how to talk to her anymore."

My heart clenched and I looked at my mom. She ran both hands over her hair, then put them on her hips.

"Your father was in town this morning and he ran into Mayor Brick," she said, looking not at me, but at the bowl of fruit on the center island. "Turns out that the Kents aren't just up here for a summer away. Robert Kent has made an offer on the old Lawrence farm." She looked up at me for the first time. "He wants to buy up all that acreage and turn it into a strip mall."

"What?" I asked, all the oxygen whooshing out of my lungs.

The Lawrence farm encompassed some of the most gorgeous property in Lake Logan, outside of the Kent place. There were old orchards, a swimming pond, and a huge hill that the kids in town used every winter for sledding. As far as I knew, Mr. Lawrence, who never had any kids, had left the farm to the town when he died. Every fall the town held this huge apple-picking weekend and people came from all over to pick bushels from the still-thriving trees, paying five bucks a pound. All the money went to the local schools for books and arts programs. It was one of my favorite Lake Logan traditions.

"Well, we're not going to let him do it," my father said. He flipped the water on in the sink and held a glass under the spout. "He thinks we need more options. A coffee shop, a deli, a *nail salon*? Who does he think he is, coming in here and telling us what we need?"

"Can you do that?" I asked, placing my bag down on the island. "Can you stop him?"

"We can definitely fight it," my mother said. "Most of the townspeople already know about it and I doubt many of them are any more thrilled than we are."

"He's going to present his plan at the town meeting later this week," my father told me. "All we have to do is rally support before then. If the whole town shows up opposed to the plan, there's no way Brick and the board can justify selling to him."

I nodded, trying to dispel the pit that had formed in my stomach. How could anyone want to tear down that orchard and replace it with an ugly strip mall? What was Jared's father thinking?

"Cassandra, I know you and your mother think that you hanging out with this Jared kid is just fine, but you have to put a stop to it," my father said, taking a swig of water from the glass. "There's no good in these people. They just walk around taking whatever they want. Doing whatever they please. Not caring about who they might hurt in the process."

"But Dad—"

"I know. You think Jared's different," he said. "But how different can he be? Children are a reflection of their parents."

"But he's nothing like his father!" I protested. "It's not fair to judge him like that. Just this morning he set up this whole picnic for me and Donna because he thought she was mad at him and he wanted to make it up to her. Does that sound like something Robert Kent would have done?"

I realized my misstep about a second after I made it. The color in my father's face, which had calmed down a bit, was now back full force.

"That's where you really were this morning? Out with the Kent kid?" he blurted.

I swallowed hard. "Yeah . . . but—"

"You spent half the year begging me and your mother to let you take on more lessons and then you just ditch them without even telling us and now you're lying about where you were?" he shouted.

"I left a note. And I didn't lie," I pointed out. "I *was* with Donna . . . ."

"Oh, that's rich. Where did you learn that? From him?" my father said sarcastically. "I guess lies of omission are all good in the city, but they're not gonna fly around here. Already this boy is having a bad influence on you."

"Dad, I'm sorry," I said. "But I wish you would just trust me on this. I'm not a little kid anymore."

"Well you sure are acting like one. Shirking your lessons . . . sneaking out of here . . . *lying*," my father said. "I want you to go get changed and get your butt down to the stable right now. Penny needs help grooming the horses. She's done enough of your work already today."

I glanced at my mother, wondering if I should even bother continuing to argue. The look on her face told me no. She was just as annoyed as my father was.

"Fine," I said. "I'll go."

I turned on my heel, frustrated, and stalked down the hallway to my room.

The next day I spent the afternoon outside under the hot sun, mowing the fields. It wasn't hard work with the tractor mower my dad had bought the summer before, and I didn't mind doing it. Especially considering it kept me out of the house and away from any more confrontation with my family. So far, this had to be the most bizarre summer of my life. I had my first kiss, my first maybe-boyfriend, my first ever friendship with invaders. But I was also fighting with my dad for the first time ever. I guess the bad really did come hand in hand with the good.

I was just turning the mower along the side of the driveway to work on the edges, when I saw a familiar SUV pull in. My heart seized up with fear, but I kept right on mowing, hoping the car would just pass me by.

What on earth was Marni Locke doing here on a Sunday afternoon? She hadn't bought extra lessons for her brats, had she?

I focused my eyes straight ahead as the SUV approached, pretending I didn't even notice it.

Please let her keep going, please let her keep going, please let her—

But the SUV stopped right behind me and before I knew it, Mrs. Locke had thrown it into reverse and was staring me down from her driver's side window. There was nothing I could do but stop the mower and deal with her. I hit the brake and killed the noisy engine.

"Tell me something," she said without so much as a hello. "Where do you get off, skipping your lessons with my sons?"

My whole chest hollowed out as I looked at her. *Good afternoon to you, too, Mrs. Locke,* I thought. *How are you today?*

Of course my tongue stayed firmly in place, cemented to the bottom of my mouth. My pulse was pounding so hard through my veins, they were throbbing. She got out of the car and slammed the door. Her white shirt was tied above her perfectly flat stomach and her capri jeans rode so low I could see the top of her pink lacy underwear.

"Correct me if I'm wrong, but I'm paying for *you* to teach my sons to ride, not some man-woman with a bad attitude," she said, whipping her sunglasses off so she could glare at me better. "You're the one who came highly recommended, though now I can hardly see why."

I swallowed against a sun-dried throat. Had Mrs. Locke really driven all the way out here on a Sunday afternoon just to ream me out? Didn't she have anything better to do? I took a deep breath and somehow screwed up my courage. "It was just one lesson," I said weakly. Great. Way to fight rudeness with timidity.

"One lesson during which my kids were

yelled at, threatened, and given a time-out for thirty minutes!" Mrs. Locke shouted, her face creasing with rage. "Thirty minutes! That's half the lesson! I'm not paying for that!"

My mind reeled. Penny had given the boys a time-out? She hadn't mentioned that yesterday when we were closing up the stable. What had they done to her?

"Well, I . . . I guess if you want your money back for that lesson you can talk to my dad. . . ."

Although he'll ground me on the spot, I thought.

"I'm not talking to your father, I'm talking to you," she snapped. "So let's get one thing straight. I expect you to be at each of my sons' lessons from here on out. If not, I'm demanding a *full* refund. Are we clear?"

My heart slammed into my ribcage. *Tell her off! Tell her that her kids are psychos! Tell her that if Penny gave them a time-out they must have done something* really *horrible.*

I stared at her beady eyes and knew I wasn't going to say any of those things. Some people have a hard time coming up with comebacks on the spot. My problem is, I come up with a ton of them, I just can't get myself to *say* anything.

"Yes," I said finally, loathing myself. "We're clear."

Just to add insult to injury, Mrs. Locke fixed me with a triumphant smile. "Good. We'll see you next weekend."

With that, she got back in her car and slammed the door. She executed a three-point turn that took her tires right over the grass, creating a nice big rut, and peeled out.

I felt awful after Mrs. Locke left. Awful and stupid and angry. I had to get out of there. I had to get Lola and go. The only thing that was going to make me feel better was a long ride. I had to clear my mind.

I rode the lawn mower back to the barn and parked it at the back, then cut across the yard to the stable. Lola was more than ready to go when I opened her stall door. It was almost as if she could sense how antsy I was. She kept shifting her weight as I put on her saddle and glancing back at me as if I weren't going fast enough.

I took her up the hill through the trees and across the Kents' meadow. After a few sprints around the field I was feeling a lot better. I imagined Mrs. Locke screaming and flailing on the back of a runaway horse and imagined Lola and myself riding up to save her . . . then passing her by. The look of total shock and fear I conjured up for her face exhilarated me. Not nice, I know, but it was just a daydream and it made my heart feel a lot lighter. Mrs. Locke wasn't better than me. She was just a mean, unhappy, bored woman who had nothing to do with her time other than yell at people half her age.

Still, I wished I could stand up to her. My father had no problem speaking his mind—shouting it when he needed to. Why hadn't I inherited that useful gene?

Finally, after about our tenth lap with Lola panting and me sweating and out of breath, I decided we had exercised enough for the afternoon. I started to turn toward home, but just thinking about going back there made my skin crawl. What was I going to do? Sulk in my room and stare at the ceiling? Endure another silent meal with my parents? I glanced to my left and had another, far more appealing idea. I pulled Lola's reins toward the east and she huffed in surprise, but went along. This wasn't a route we took very often anymore.

We found the path in the woods through which Jared had exploded the first morning we met him. I knew my father wanted me to stay away from Jared, but I just couldn't. Not with the way he made me feel. And besides, I didn't agree with my father's reasoning. I knew Jared, and he was nothing like his father.

Lola and I clopped carefully along the path's twists and turns, winding our way down the far side of the hill. At the bottom we emerged on the periphery of the Kents' backyard. The house loomed up in the distance, behind the cabana, the garage, and the pool.

Feeling exhilarated, I took Lola around to the right, hugging the tree line just in case Jared's parents spotted us and we had to make a quick break for it. I looked up at the many windows at the back of the house, wondering if Jared was home. Which window led to his bedroom? Did he even have just one, or had he been assigned several rooms in the massive house, like a prince?

Everything was quiet and still. We were nearing the side of the house and I was just about to turn Lola around and head back when I saw something move out of the corner of my eye. My heart gave a massive start, but I relaxed instantly when I saw that it was just Jared. He was sitting up straight in a lounge chair by the pool, waving me down.

"Hey! Trespassers! What are you doing here?" he called.

"Uh . . . trespassing?" I joked.

"Come on over!" Jared said, pushing himself up. "No one's home. I promise I won't press charges," he added with a heart-stopping smile.

I laughed and trotted Lola across the lawn. An iron fence ran around the pool area. I jumped down and tethered her to one of the posts. Jared walked over and opened a gate for me.

"Hey. This is a nice surprise," he said.

Then, much to my delight, he leaned down and planted a kiss on my lips. I sighed.

"I knew coming here would make me feel better," I said, stepping onto the flagstones that surrounded the pool. The water glistened in the sinking sun. On the far side of the pool, a hot tub bubbled away. Jared had a pitcher of iced tea laid out on the table next to his chair and a

Maxim magazine folded out on the ground.

"I read it for the articles," he joked, noticing my furrowed brow. "So why do you need to feel better?"

We walked over to the dozen or so cushy lounge chairs and sat down. I groaned and leaned my forearms on my thighs.

"This . . . *woman*, Mrs. Locke," I told him. "She came over today just to tell me off for missing yesterday's lesson with her monster children."

"You're kidding," he said, handing me his half-full glass of iced tea. I took a long sip and sighed as the cool liquid quenched my exercise-induced thirst.

"No, but that's not the worst part," I told him, flushing. "She was yelling at me and I just sat there and took it. I could have told her how evil her kids are or pointed out that everyone's entitled to one day off. I could have just told her what an incredible bitch she is, but I didn't."

"Why not?" he asked. "Sounds like she deserves it, coming over just to attack you in the middle of the weekend."

"I know! I just . . . couldn't," I said, deflating. "I can't stand up to people. I'm just . . . so bad at it."

Jared leaned back on his hands. "You stood up to me on the first day we met," he said.

"Yeah, but that was different," I said.

"Why?"

"Because you were just an obnoxious guy who needed knocking down a few pegs," I told him, smiling.

Jared grinned. "Oh really?"

"Yes, really," I replied. "Trust me, if I had met your dad up there instead of you and *he* had accused me of trespassing, I would have pretty much fainted right there."

"Well, I'm glad it was me, then," Jared said, sitting up. He reached out and took my hand, holding it between us. My skin tingled all the way up my arm as he toyed with my fingers. "But seriously, Gracie. You can't let people walk all over you. They're just people. What right do they have?"

I swallowed back a lump in my throat and stared at the ground. When he put it that simply, I felt like even more of a moron.

"Speaking of your father," I said, wanting to change the subject. "What's up with this whole strip mall thing he apparently wants to build here?"

Jared's face seemed to shut down. He dropped my hand and looked away, across the pool. "Actually, I don't really talk about my dad's work with him," he said, picking up his magazine and fiddling with it.

"But you've heard about it," I pressed.

"Yeah, I guess I heard something."

"Well, it's a really bad idea," I told him. "None of the townspeople are going to want it. So if he says anything to you about it—"

"Like I said, we don't really talk about his work," Jared said, cutting me off. I blinked, surprised, but before I could think of anything else to say, he was on his feet. He rolled up the magazine into a tube and squeezed. "You want to come inside? I can show you around."

I felt a zip of excitement at the idea of stepping inside the Kent mansion and the strip mall was temporarily forgotten. This place had always loomed mysteriously over the town like a haunted house or a royal palace or Willy

Wonka's chocolate factory. Fascinating, but untouchable.

"Sure," I said.

He held out his hand again and I took it with a smile, feeling better already. As he opened the gate for me and led me over to the screened-in back porch that ran the length of the house, I wished my father could see us together. How bad could Jared be if he didn't want me to let people walk all over me? If he held my hand and opened doors for me and made me feel better when I was down in the dumps?

"Cassie Grace," he said, opening the back door. "Welcome to Casa Kent."

Chapter Fifteen

The Kent house was even more unbelievable than I had ever imagined. I knew I was in for it when I saw that the back porch, with its leaf-shaped ceiling fans, cushy lounges, and hardwood floor, was nicer than any regular room in my own house. As Jared led me through the back hall and the tremendous kitchen (bigger than the one at my high school; it had an actual pizza oven built into a brick wall), I had to bite my tongue to keep from oohing and ahhing like I was in a museum. They may as well have opened the place up and charged admission. Not only would everyone in town come to check it out, but it would be worth the ticket price.

"So this is the front foyer," Jared said,

pausing in a huge, two-story room. "This is where you would be if you came in the front door." His voice echoed off the high walls and gleaming stone floor. Up above, a huge, modern chandelier defied all laws of gravity, suspended from the center of the ceiling. It was made of raw iron that had been twisted to look like intertwining branches and leaves.

"What's in there?" I asked, pointing at the closed doors to my left.

"It's a drawing room, whatever that means, and behind that is my father's study," Jared said. "There's a couple of rooms back there that never see the light of day. A library, some kind of 'smoking room' . . ." he said, throwing in some air quotes. "Unfortunately, no one in this family smokes."

"What about that one?"

Jared turned to the other pair of closed doors and smiled. "That is one of my favorite rooms. Check it out."

He slid the doors apart and stood aside. My breath was nearly taken away by the sheer size of the room—and of everything in it. Plus, the décor was not at all what you would expect in an old Victorian. It looked as if the decorator had been commissioned off one of those movies from my mother's childhood that she's always taping off TBS—*Pretty in Pink* or *Less than Zero* or something. A black lacquer dining table that could seat at least twenty-four people stretched out in front of me, ending in front of a wide stone fireplace. The chairs around it were tall and black, but asymmetrical, each one with a geometrically distinct back. To the left of the table was a long window with hundreds of tiny panes that looked out over the front yard. A lacquer breakfront to the right took up almost the entire wall, displaying china plates and tea cups in intricate, modern patterns. The floor was a gleaming white tile and the walls were deep red.

"Disgusting, isn't it?" Jared said gleefully. "My parents argue about this room almost every day. My mother loves it. My father wants to burn it down. It's the Kent family standoff."

"It's crazy," I agreed. "I feel like I stepped into a time warp."

"My mother decorated it in the late eighties or something, back when my parents actually thought they were going to use this place," Jared said, stepping inside and leaning against the chair at the head of the table. "She apparently sent workers up here every weekend and had them take pictures of their progress and bring them back."

"Ah. The days before the Internet," I joked.

"Yeah, right?" Jared said. "My dad wants to redo it, but my mom freaks every time he mentions it. She says she worked her butt off on it and never got to enjoy it so now she wants it the way it is."

He rolled his eyes and looked at the ceiling, where a gaudy, colorful light sculpture hung.

"Do your parents fight a lot?" I asked, then immediately wondered if he was going to be offended.

"Not really," he said matter-of-factly. "Just lately. What about yours?"

I sighed, thinking of the arguments over me and Jared and the Kents in general. "Just lately," I echoed.

"Sucks, right?" Jared said.

I looked him in the eye and suddenly felt like hugging him, but I held back. I wasn't sure we were at the random hugging phase, if there was one. "Yeah."

"Wanna check out upstairs?" Jared asked, completely changing his tone.

My heart thumped extra hard. I assumed his bedroom was up there somewhere, and here we were alone in the house. . . . The responsible girl in me told me to keep to the downstairs tour, just so there were no mixed messages. But the girl who really liked and trusted Jared and had nowhere else to go won out.

"Sure," I said.

The wide staircase stood in a grand hall behind the foyer. The entire house was silent as we made our way upstairs. The second-floor hallway curled around to the right and left with a third hall dead ahead. At the very end of that, another, smaller staircase turned off to the right, leading up to the third floor. The only light came from dim sconces lit on the walls, casting shadows on the classic striped wallpaper. We paused at the crossroads.

"Well, I can either show you about a half dozen boring guest rooms, or I can just get it over with and show you my room," Jared said, knocking his hands together. "But I have to warn you, if you see my room, you may leave this house and never talk to me again."

I blinked. "Why?"

Jared tipped his head back and groaned. "Screw it. You're going to find out sooner or later."

I was intrigued and a little disturbed as I followed him off to the right, around a corner, and down the hallway. He paused in front of a door on the left side of the hall.

"All right, you have to promise not to judge me," Jared said, grasping the doorknob.

"Oooookay," I said.

Jared sighed and opened the door onto complete and utter chaos. Like every other room in the house, Jared's bedroom was cavernous. But unlike every other room, it was also a complete wreck. Clothing hung from every available surface, including what appeared to be a regulation-size basketball net on the far wall. A crushed pizza box on the floor sat under a half-empty jug of fruit punch Gatorade. There were wrappers and cans and bottles and paper bags everywhere. A pile of used dishes sat on top of his desk, cheese congealing to the surface of the top one, which looked like it would topple off with one good shake of the floor. His bed was, of course, unmade and the pillows were on the floor, one of them with a corner in a cereal bowl half filled with milk. A huge TV stood on the wall across from the bed and speakers hung in every corner. These seemed to be the only items in the room that had escaped the destruction.

"Wow. You're disgusting," I said matter-of-factly. "You do realize you've only been here for a couple of weeks."

"I know," Jared said. "It wouldn't be this bad, but my dad told the cleaning lady never to come in here. It's his way of punishing me for making such a stink about coming up here. He said no one's cleaning it but me until I apologize for some things I said."

He walked over and whipped his comforter, showering clothing off of it onto the floor on the far side of the bed. Then he smoothed it out, clearing a space for me to sit.

"So . . . you've just decided to live in filth instead of cleaning it yourself," I said.

"It's kind of a protest statement," Jared

said, placing his hands on his hips and looking around with satisfaction, like he was a farmer surveying his fields.

"Um . . . but you do realize that you're the only one who suffers, right?" I said, trying not to stare at an unidentifiable stain on the rug.

Jared looked at me. "You may have a point." Then he turned and clapped his hands together. "Anyway, I did not bring you up here to talk about my disgustingness."

"I'm not sure that's a word," I joked.

He headed over to the stereo and punched a few buttons. "It's my house. I can make up words if I want to," he said over his shoulder. "I brought you up here to let you in on a little Jared Kent ritual."

"What's that?" I asked. I was going to lean back on the bed, but instead crossed my arms over my stomach. Who knew what I would lean into?

"C'mere," he said, raising his eyebrows and wagging his fingers at me.

Once again, my pulse was racing. I joined him over by the basketball hoop, where the only mess was some tangled clothing and a pile of old CDs. From the wide bay window you could see out over the pool and most of the backyard. Lola stood patiently tethered to the fence, watching the woods.

"What are we doing?" I asked.

"I am going to help you take out your frustration about that Locke person. Whenever I get annoyed or feel trapped, there's one thing that always makes me feel better," he said.

"What's that?" I asked, smirking.

Jared reached over and punched a button on the stereo. The entire room exploded with noise and Jared started bouncing around like a maniac, flailing his arms and banging his head. I cracked up laughing and pressed my fingers over my ears.

"What *is* this?" I shouted.

"It's punk! *Vintage* punk," he shouted back, bouncing up and down on the balls of his feet. "Come on! Get into it! I swear it'll make you feel better!"

It took a couple seconds, but I quickly got used to the volume and was even able to distinguish the beat. Jared jumped around in front of me, kicking clothes out of the way, laughing and making a complete ass out of himself. How he could still look cute while he spazzed out was totally beyond me. Finally, he got fed up with my nonparticipation and grabbed my hands.

"Come on!" he shouted.

I laughed and blushed, but started mirroring his movements. When he jumped, I jumped. He kicked and I kicked. Pretty soon I forgot where I was and who I was with. I even forgot why my heart had felt so heavy when I had ridden over here. We danced and twirled and flailed around his room until I was sweating and out of breath. Until I was laughing so hard my gut hurt.

Toward the end of the song the guitar went crazy repetitive, jamming the same chord over and over and over again. Jared grabbed my hands and spun me around, blurring the room so that all I could focus on was his grin. I screamed as I almost lost my footing and then finally the song ended and we both tumbled onto his bed, dizzy and laughing and gasping for air.

"Feel better?" Jared asked, his chest heaving up and down.

I nodded. "Yeah. I might throw up, but yeah."

"I have a better idea," Jared said.

Then he turned on his side, propped himself up on his shoulder and kissed me. And suddenly, the room was spinning for a whole new reason.

Two days later, I found myself for the first time in the same room with Jared's father. It wasn't at the Kents' house, however, and as far as I knew he wasn't even aware that I existed, let alone that I was there. He was probably a little more interested in the hundred or so angry adults who packed the meeting room at the town hall, salivating for his head.

All the town meetings, plus the Elks Club meetings, the School Board meetings, the local AA meetings and the Women's Club meetings were all held in the smallish meeting room at the town hall. It was a fluorescent-lit, wood-paneled room with a permanent cigarette smoke smell that pretty much sucked the color out of your skin and made you drowsy the moment you walked in. I had only been there once before when my friends and I had lobbied the School Board for an eighth grade dance. They had shot us down, only to start one up a year later. It takes every governing entity in this town at least twelve months to make a decision about anything. Mr. Kent had no idea what he was in for.

Still, he looked relatively calm and unaffected as he took his front-row seat in one of the ancient folding chairs facing the long table where the mayor and his lackeys sat. I had been expecting Mr. Kent to show up looking all Trump-like in a designer suit with a briefcase. Instead he sat there in an open-necked white shirt and khakis with a plain blue folder in his lap. And he still looked more distinguished than any other man in the room.

"All right, all right! Let's settle down." Mayor Brick called out, slamming a gavel on the faux wood surface of the metal table a few times.

The din in the room fell to a whisper as people took their seats. The room was filled to capacity, with more concerned citizens lining the walls. Actually, I wasn't sure they were so much concerned citizens as people hoping for a glimpse of Robert Kent and his family. Unfortunately for them, Jared and his mother were nowhere in sight. I wondered how they could stay away. This meeting was all the town had talked about for the past few days. But then again, they weren't exactly part of the town. I was disappointed not to see Jared, though. At this point, he was pretty much all I thought about and I would have taken any chance I could get to see him.

Of course, he had dodged the strip mall subject pretty handily that day at his house. Apparently he really did have zero interest in his father's work.

I myself had come out of sheer thirst for drama. Lake Logan hadn't seen this much excitement since . . . well . . . not since before I was born.

My father sat next to me, his face stoic, his arms crossed over his broad chest. Mom was next to him, sitting on the edge of her seat. Across the aisle from me were Donna and her family, and she winked at me as she fell into her chair next to Derek. That afternoon we had finally squeezed in our shopping trip and I noticed that she was already sporting the embroidered jeans she had purchased. All my stuff, meanwhile, had been packed into the back of my closet, not to be touched until I got to college.

"Okay, normally we would read the minutes from last week and go on to the business we've had planned for a while now, but I know you all aren't here to listen to any of that," Mayor Brick said, drawing a few laughs. He pulled up the waistband of his pants under his round belly and smiled, proud of his joke. His silver hair gleamed under the lights and I had a feeling he'd used more product than usual, knowing he was going to have an audience. "So let's get right on to the task at hand. Robert Kent has made a generous offer on the old Lawrence place and proposes to build a strip mall on the premises."

There was an angry murmur through the crowd and I glanced at Mr. Kent. His expression didn't change a bit. He was cool as a cucumber, his attention focused on the mayor. This guy was good.

"Now I'm going to let Mr. Kent come up here and share a brief outline of his proposal with you, and then we'll hear comments from the floor," Mayor Brick said. "Mr. Kent?"

Mayor Brick sat down behind the table and Mr. Kent got up. My father stiffened in the seat next to me. Instead of striding to the center of the room and standing directly in front of the mayor, Mr. Kent stayed in his corner and addressed the audience. Up close, he looked older than I thought. His hair was thin and graying, especially around the temples, and the skin on his face was a little slack, like someone who had recently been hit with the stomach flu. As he stood he was met with jeers and boos and for a second, I was embarrassed to be there. So none of us wanted to see the Lawrence farm go. Did the adults in the room have to act like second graders about it?

"My proposal calls for a strip mall with ten storefronts and one large warehouse-style space for a supermarket, along with one hundred parking spaces," Mr. Kent began.

"A hundred parking spaces?" someone behind me muttered. "We don't even have a hundred cars in this town."

Everyone around the jokester laughed.

"The façade of the mall would be rustic and tasteful to fit in with the environs," Mr. Kent continued unfazed. "And the plans would call for the razing of the farmhouse and outbuildings, but would only affect about a third of the orchard."

This got a rousing protest from the audience, which I could tell Mr. Kent was surprised about. He clearly thought that saving any of the orchard was a benevolent move on his part. Still, he gamely continued over the growing noise.

"With reasonable rents and generous spaces, this mall would give area professionals a chance to open small businesses and restaurants without the cost of building their own structures," Mr. Kent said. "It will create jobs and give all of you a new variety of shopping and dining choices, which I, for one, think the people of this town deserve."

He glanced over at the mayor, who was looking on with a disturbing amount of interest.

"That's it for me," Mr. Kent finished with a smile. "Thanks for your time."

"Who are you to decide what we deserve?" someone in the back of the room shouted.

Instantly the room erupted in chaos. Shouts and jeers and questions and feet stomping.

Mayor Brick almost broke his gavel trying to get everyone back to order. Donna rolled her eyes at me and made a big show of pulling out her latest summer romance novel.

"I'd like to say something!" my father said, standing just as the noise died down. I felt sick to my stomach as every pair of eyes in the room turned toward us.

"The chair recognizes Thomas Grace," the mayor said, looking relieved.

"I'm not sure how you know what we do or don't deserve, Mr. Kent, being that you haven't set foot in this town in twenty years," my father said, staring him down.

A smattering of applause and cheers met his statement, but my father held up a hand, instantly silencing it.

"But what we *want* is to preserve our way of life," my father continued. "We have traditions around here. Traditions that are important to us. History that we want our kids to be a part of. Now I wouldn't expect a man like you to understand that, but understand this: You can't just come in here and destroy that because you want some more green to line your pockets.

We won't let you do it."

I swallowed hard as the room exploded again. A few people even gave my father a standing ovation. I, for one, felt ill. My father had just insulted Jared's father to his face. Now I was kind of glad Jared hadn't shown.

Mr. Kent stood up. "If tradition and history are your priorities, I do have a counter proposal," he shouted, quieting everyone.

"Uh . . . the chair recognizes Robert Kent," Mayor Brick said.

"Let's hear it," my father said with a touch of sarcasm. Whatever it was, he was going to shoot it down.

"If the town council approves the sale of the Lawrence land to me, I will, in turn, finance the restoration of a great town landmark, the Regency Theater."

A universal gasp went out over the room. Donna dropped her book. Derek went pale. Suddenly, their father and mother were sitting straight up in their seats.

"What?" Donna's dad blurted.

My heart fluttered painfully in my chest. The Policastros had been trying to figure out a way to restore the Regency to its former glory for years, but had never been able to get the financing together. I knew that it was Donna's father's dream to see the old place brought back to the way his dad had imagined it. For a guy who didn't seem to know much about us Lake Loganers, Robert Kent had just hit upon the deepest wish of one of our favorite towns-people.

"I, for one, would love to see the elegance and glitz of the old place restored," Mr. Kent said, breaking the stunned silence. "Together we can bring it back to the way it used to be. I've looked into the history of the place and learned that it was one of the first movie houses built in upstate New York. I propose a full overhaul and restoration and I myself will lobby the state for landmark status so that the building will be pro-tected from future development. That is, if my other offer is accepted."

Everyone was whispering and shifting. I gaped at Donna, who gaped at her parents. Derek looked like he was about to faint out of his chair.

"This is ridiculous," my father said finally.

"It's a bribe! He thinks he can just buy us all off."

"Now, now, Thomas. I think I'd like to hear what the owners of the theater have to say about this proposal," Mayor Brick said. Everyone in the room looked at Donna's parents. "Jim? Lucy?" Mayor Brick said.

Donna's dad shifted in his seat, cleared his throat and sat up straight. "I'd . . . be willing to listen."

After that, you couldn't have gotten the room under control with a nuclear explosion.

Chapter Sixteen

*O*ddly enough, there were no protest rallies staged in the next few days and things were relatively normal, except that everywhere you went people were debating about what should be done. *My* parents, of course, became completely obsessed. They spent half their time calling up friends and townspeople, trying to rally support against the strip mall, as if there were anyone in town who hadn't heard about it through the normal gossip channels. Apparently a vote was going to be taken in the near future, although I couldn't get a straight answer about when that would actually take place. I had a feeling that a lot of people thought that if they put it off long enough, maybe Robert Kent would go back to the city and forget all about us.

Luckily, my parents were so distracted that they didn't even notice that Penny was taking on more of my students. Somewhere in the back of my mind, I knew that I was supposed to be making money for my entrance fee, but I always seemed to forget about that when Jared called up to propose a trip to the make-out beach or a drive up to the mountains for a picnic. Being with Jared, in fact, made me forget about a lot of things. Whenever we were together, I stopped thinking about the strip mall and the competition—even about the fact that I was heading to college in the fall.

All that mattered to me when Jared was around was Jared. One afternoon he even did manage to get me on his motorcycle. And I have to say, it was one of the more exhilarating experiences of my life.

When people in town asked me about my feelings on the Lawrence farm, which they inevitably did, I told them the truth—that I had absolutely no idea how to feel about that matter. On the one hand, Donna's dad was psyched beyond belief about the idea of renovating the theater and drawing more people from neighboring towns. Donna and her family would definitely benefit from that. On the other, I loved the yearly Apple Festival and that brought the entire town a lot of money and tourism. So everyone benefited from that.

What was a small-town girl to do?

The week after the town meeting, I went to pick up Donna in the truck for a double date with Jared and Christopher. I was relishing the thought of a few hours clear of the strip mall debate. Jared and I hadn't talked about it since he put a lid on the subject by the pool, and I knew Donna wouldn't bring it up, as it had taken over her household even more completely than it had taken over mine. In fact, Donna and Derek were locked in a battle of wills about everyone's favorite subject even as I walked through their front door, their voices echoing from the kitchen at the back of the house.

"Hey guys! It's me!" I shouted.

There was a clang as someone tossed some dishes into the sink and then a bang as someone slammed a cabinet door.

"God, Derek! You are so thick!" Donna shouted, stalking out of the kitchen and down the hallway toward me. She grabbed her bag from the bottom stair in front of me and reached around me for the door. "Don't you even care about the theater?"

"Of course I do! But who does he think he is?" Derek replied, his face a raging red as he followed after her. "He acts like this benevolent savior, swooping in here to bail our family out when Cassie's dad was right!" he said, thrusting a hand in my direction. "He *is* just trying to buy us all off! He thinks he's going to look all saintly by helping us out and everyone's just going to fall all over him in thanks."

"Could you be any more cynical?" Donna asked, crossing her arms over her chest.

"Could *you* be any more naive?" Derek shot back, mimicking her pose.

Sometimes I was jealous of Donna and Derek's close relationship and wished I had a brother or sister to hang out with. This was not one of those times.

Donna clucked her tongue and Derek looked us up and down as if he were seeing us for the first time. I was wearing a pair of old but flattering riding pants and Donna had on jeans, even though it was eighty-five degrees out.

"Where're you guys going?" Derek asked.

"Riding," I replied. "With Jared and Christopher."

He was going to find out sooner or later.

"Oh, that's great!" Derek said, throwing his hands up. "Dad's up all night trying to figure out what to do and you two are sleeping with the enemy."

"Ugh!" Donna exclaimed.

"We are not *sleeping* with anyone!" I added, flushing.

"It's an expression," Derek said. Then he narrowed his eyes. "But you'd better not be."

"Look, Derek. Christopher and Jared are *not* the enemy," Donna said flatly. "And whatever Jared's father's motives are, wouldn't it be great to have the theater renovated? I mean, come on, it's all Mom and Dad have talked about since we were zygotes."

Derek stood up straight and crossed his arms over his chest. "So they'll do it themselves," he said.

Donna rolled her eyes. "Yeah, because they've gotten so far with that plan up 'til now." She whipped the door open and traipsed out, leaving Derek slack-jawed behind her.

"I guess we're going," I said to him, shrugging by way of apology.

"Cassie," he said, stopping me in my tracks.

"Yeah?"

He took a couple of steps toward me and looked me dead in the eye. "Just look after her, okay? She never thinks before she jumps."

I smiled slightly. Even in the middle of a knock-down, drag-out fight, Derek never stopped being the overprotective brother.

"I got it," I said. "Don't worry, all right? Christopher's fine. He's a nice guy."

"Well I hope so, 'cuz all she's been talking about for the past twenty-four hours is the dance," he said.

My heart took a nose dive. "The dance. You mean *the* dance? The Summer Fling?"

"Yep." It was the grimmest "yep" in the history of "yep"s.

"Did he ask her?" I would have been shocked if Christopher had asked Donna to the annual country club dance and she hadn't told me. It was the biggest invader event of the year and locals were hardly ever asked. When they were, it was usually because they were, for lack of a better word, sluts. Everyone knew what an invader wanted from a local on the night of the Summer Fling. And I couldn't imagine that Donna was willing to give that to Christopher. She barely even knew the guy!

"Not yet. But she obviously wants him to," Derek told me. My relief must have shown on my face, because he added, "He must not be such a nice guy if you're that happy they're not going."

"No! Not at all!" I protested. "I just know they're not that serious. She's probably just being Donna. Daydreams are her life."

He shrugged slightly at the truth of this.

"Don't worry. Really," I told him. "It's just a harmless little fling."

"Yeah," he said, glancing past me out the door, where Donna was checking her lip gloss in the truck's side mirror. "But a fling is only harmless for the person who doesn't get flung."

* * *

When Christopher had told Donna that he and Jared wanted to go out for a ride with us, she had called up Rianne Conroy at Saddle Up Stables in Morganville. It was a half hour drive from Lake Logan, but considering how my dad was feeling about the Kents, Donna had rightly assumed that I wouldn't want to take the guys riding on our property. Rianne was a cool woman who knew everything there was to know about horses. Her stable was written up in all the tourism guides as the place to go for guided rides into the mountains, and she did a good business. She often bought old nags and runts off my dad for the tourists to ride. The last thing she needed was to put some middle-aged chiropractor from Philly on a purebred and have the horse go on a tear. She liked to keep things safe and simple.

A good thing, since Jared and Christopher proved to be even more clueless about horses than I had been about a stick shift.

"All right, you're all set," Rianne said, leading the last of four horses, a yellow nag named Buttercup, out of the stable. I had named her myself when I was a kid and she was a foal in our stable. Rianne brought Buttercup over to

Christopher and handed him the reins.

"What's his name?" Christopher asked.

I opened my mouth to answer, but Rianne cut me off. "Lightning," she told him with a sly smile in my direction.

"Aw, yeah!" Christopher said. "Just my style."

I grinned and looked away, hiding my smile as I tightened the tack on Jared's horse, Whisper. Clearly Rianne knew her clientele.

"I'd tell you to be careful out there, girls, but I know I can trust ya," Rianne said, swinging her long dark hair over her shoulder. "Just have 'em back by four. I got a family from Buffalo coming in."

"You got it, Rianne," Donna said. She fed her horse, Lucky, a carrot, then ran her hand down his snout. Rianne headed back into the stables and I turned to Jared.

"You ready to do this?" I asked him.

"Yeah, Kent. You first," Christopher said.

Jared stepped up next to Whisper and looked up uncertainly. "He's a lot bigger than I expected."

"Afraid of heights?" I teased.

"Please. Kent's not afraid of anything," Christopher said.

"All right, then," I said, pulling out the stirrup. "Put your right foot in here, grab the horn on the saddle, and give yourself a good boost up. All you have to do is swing your left leg over and settle in."

Jared's brow creased in concentration and he did exactly as he was told. In one impressively smooth motion he was sitting in the saddle like an old pro. The grin on his face was infectious.

"You sure you haven't done this before?" Donna asked him.

"That's Kent. He's good at everything," Christopher said with a smirk.

"I think you have a fan," I said under my breath.

Jared just laughed.

Getting Christopher up in the saddle was a bit more difficult and a lot more entertaining. The first time, he went up and fell right back down on his butt, not giving himself enough momentum. The second time, he tipped forward onto his stomach and ended up gripping the horse's mane with both feet in the air until he slid back down again. Donna tried her best not to laugh as she helped him up. Buttercup looked back at him like, "What the heck have you saddled me with?"

"Come on, man. Get up there," Jared said as Christopher set up for his third attempt. "Just give yourself a good push."

Christopher smoothed both hands through his curly hair and, with a look of complete determination, swung himself up and into the saddle. This time he almost gave himself *too* good of a push and he started to slide down the other side of the saddle. Donna ran around and gripped his hand, pushing him back up.

"Whoo! That wasn't so bad," Christopher said, sitting straight in the saddle now.

Jared and I clapped for him as Donna saddled up on Lucky. "Nice work," Jared said.

"All right. So how fast does this puppy go?" Christopher asked, looking around as if he were trying to find the ignition.

I looked at Jared and rolled my eyes, grinning, as I mounted my horse, Joe Cool. This was going to be an interesting afternoon.

"I love this view," Donna said, gazing out over the trees and the higher mountain tops. We were standing at the clearing on St. Michael's peak, the top of the trail we had chosen to show the guys.

"Yeah. It's great," Christopher said flatly. "Now can we go back down to the field? I want to open this baby up and see what he can do."

Donna snorted a laugh. "Uh, Christopher, maybe you should master moseying first before you try for a full-out gallop."

"What? How hard could it be?" Christopher asked. He pulled on Buttercup's reins and tried to turn her as Donna and I had instructed, but instead of turning and moving forward Buttercup backed up into Whisper, who sashayed to the side with an irritated snort.

"Whoa, whoa," Jared said, patting Whisper's neck. "He's just a moron. Don't worry about him."

Donna and I laughed, but Christopher shot him a look of death. "Whatever. I'm going back down."

He dug his heels into Buttercup's sides and she gave a lurch before heading back toward the path downhill at a slow pace. Donna shook her head gleefully and followed.

"Wait up, John Wayne!" she said, trotting to catch up.

"That guy is all about speed," Jared said with a mock-reproving sigh.

"Oh, and you're not," I said.

"Not on this thing," Jared told me, then winked. "Not yet, anyway."

He clicked his tongue, gave Whisper a little squeeze, and turned to follow after our friends. Honestly, it was as if he had been on a horse all his life. Or, at the very least, longer than one afternoon. Was there nothing this guy couldn't do?

"So you've really never ridden before?" I asked Jared, catching up with him. I slowed my horse's steps as we drew up alongside Whisper. Jared's posture was perfect. He leaned back slightly as we started downhill, something that I normally had to teach people to do.

"Only this one embarrassing night when I needed a ride home," he joked.

I laughed. "That seems like a million years ago already."

"Yeah. I barely even knew you then," he said.

"Oh, and you know me so well now?" I joked.

"Well, I know *more*," he replied with a mischievous smile. "I know how much your riding means to you. I know that you hate fighting with your father. I know how you like to be kissed. . . ."

"Jared!" I said, blushing furiously.

He grinned at me and thankfully didn't press the subject. It wasn't like I could have an informed conversation about kissing, being that he was the only person I had ever kissed. But I definitely liked the way he did it. Sometimes, it was all I could think about.

Like now, for instance.

Up ahead, Donna laughed and I saw the way she looked at Christopher. Whatever I had said earlier about a fling may have been premature. From that pleased flush and those wide eyes, the girl had it bad.

"So, what do you think about those two?" I

asked, lifting my chin.

Jared shrugged. "They're good together," he said. "Christopher's having fun. He told me he really likes her."

"Does he? Good," I said, feeling relieved.

"What about you?" Jared asked.

"*What* about me?" I asked.

"Are you having fun?" he asked with that heart-fluttering little half smile.

"Definitely," I replied.

"Good," Jared said, looking ahead. "So am I."

"Really? Even though you're not in the Hamptons?" I teased.

"Hamptons, schmamptons," he said. "I got my best friend. I got a horse. I got a beautiful girl at my side. Who needs the Hamptons?"

One stiff breeze would have knocked me right off my horse. "Beautiful? Really?" I squeaked, then was instantly embarrassed.

But Jared just grinned over at me. "If you don't know that by now, then the guys around here have been seriously slacking."

"The guys around here wouldn't know beauty if it walked up and licked their face,"

Donna called back over her shoulder.

My stomach turned. I hadn't realized how close we had gotten to them. Had they really heard every word of what Jared and I were saying?

Donna and Christopher laughed, but I didn't have long to be mortified. Soon we came to the end of the trail and stepped out onto the field that we would need to cross to get back to Saddle Up Stables. We could see the stable buildings up ahead and a couple of SUVs parked outside. Apparently the family from Buffalo had already arrived.

"I think we're a little late," Donna said, checking her watch.

"All the more reason to giddy-up," Christopher said, looking psyched. He leaned forward in his saddle and before I could even blink, he'd let out a totally ridiculous "Yee-ha!"

"Uh . . . Christopher?" Donna said.

"No!" I said.

But it was too late. He had already dug his heels into Buttercup's sides and she had taken off at a trot. Not a sprint, not a run, but a trot — not exactly fast. Still, Christopher bounced up and down in the saddle like a rag doll tied to a dog's back. I could only imagine what would happen if Buttercup had actually decided to sprint. I had a feeling we'd have one broken neck on our hands.

"Uhhhhh!" Christopher shouted, clinging to the horn on his saddle. His voice went in and out as he popped up and down. His head whipped around as if his neck had jellified. Total whiplash. "Someone! A little help!"

Donna, Jared, and I cracked up laughing. I couldn't help it. The big, tough-guy athlete looked so silly on a wildly *trotting* horse, shouting for help.

"I guess I should put him out of his misery," Donna said. She nudged Lucky forward and easily caught up with Christopher, grabbing his horse's reins. The moment Donna pulled Buttercup up, Christopher collapsed forward and slid down to the ground on shaky legs.

"Wow. That was totally pathetic," Jared said, raising his eyebrows.

"Just goes to show," I said. "Speed is not always the answer."

* * *

I was in such a good mood when I got home from our ride that, for once, I wasn't even thinking about the stalemate between me and my father. Jared had enjoyed himself so much that he had asked me if I would take him out again this weekend. He really wanted to learn how to ride. Christopher, of course, was a lot less enthusiastic, but Donna had seemed to enjoy nursing his bruised ego all the way back to Jared's house and the two of them had shared a serious kiss good-bye. It looked like both Donna and I had found romance this summer—which was a lot more than either of us had been expecting. So when I saw my father sitting at the kitchen table, poring over some bills, it didn't even occur to me to think anything was up.

"Hey, Dad!" I said, going to the refrigerator for some juice.

"Cassie," he said by way of greeting. He peered down at the paper in front of him and added casually, "Another day of leisure?"

I held my breath and stared stoically into the fridge. There was no way I was going to let him ruin my natural high. Not today. Today everything had been perfect and I wasn't going to let my father's all-work-and-no-play attitude erase that.

"Just the afternoon, actually," I said, grabbing a bottle of apple juice and shaking it—hard. "I did all my chores this morning and I had a really good lesson with Melissa Manning. She's definitely coming along."

I walked over and leaned back against the center island. Part of me wanted to just flee back to my bedroom, but I was tired of running off like a little kid whenever he got mad. Maybe if I kept the conversation light he would let it go. Whatever it was he was annoyed about.

"That's good, but I wouldn't say you did *all* your chores," he said, placing the page down and glancing up at me.

I wracked my brain, going over the morning and trying to figure out what I could have forgotten to do. But the stalls had been mucked out and hosed down. The horses brushed and fed. I had even reorganized the lesson tack for good measure, so that the stable would even *look* tidier.

"What?" I asked him finally.

"You were supposed to help your mother

and me mend the fence at the far end of the corral, remember?" he said.

I closed my eyes, feeling like a forgetful idiot. We had talked about this last night at dinner and I had completely spaced. It hadn't even popped into my mind that morning when Donna had called to make plans. I heard "Jared" and "Christopher" and "riding" and suddenly everything else apparently shut down.

"Look, I realize that you've been ignoring my advice and running around with that Kent kid anyway. And I've chosen to ignore it because you are, as you've pointed out, an adult," my father said sternly. "But when it starts getting in the way of your work, I am going to say something. You have responsibilities around here, Cassie, and I expect you to fulfill them."

I felt beyond snagged at his perfect assessment of the situation with Jared. It wasn't as if I thought he was totally blind and ignorant, but I suppose I had thought I had been getting away with *some* of it.

"I'm sorry," I told him, feeling guilty. "I'll do it tomorrow."

"You sure will," he said, fixing me with his

patented glare. "Because tomorrow you are going to stay home all day and work."

I stood up straight. Was he grounding me? "All day? But I'm supposed to meet Jared tomorrow afternoon at Pete's. He's going to introduce me to some of his other friends."

"Not tomorrow, he's not," he said.

"Dad!"

"I'm sorry, but you have too much to catch up on, Cassie," he snapped. "Things that are more important than rubbing elbows with the summer locals."

The acidity of his tone could have rusted metal. Dad *really* hated the invaders right now. A lot more than usual.

"What do you mean, 'too much to catch up on'?" I asked.

"It's not just the fence that's fallen by the wayside while you run around fulfilling your new social calendar," my father said. "Your room is a mess. This kitchen needs a scrub down, which, if I'm not mistaken, is a job we pay you allowance to do. You haven't worked Lola out in days—"

"Yes I have!" I protested.

"Riding her over to that Kent place is not working her out," my father snapped. "When was the last time you two did a full jumping practice?"

I shut my mouth and looked away. He had me there. I couldn't even remember when the fences and jumps had been set up out on the paddock.

"It's one day, Cassandra," he said, sounding weary. "If you can't give this place and that horse one day of your time, then I don't even know why you're bothering entering that competition. If you can't give us that, then all the hard work you've done over the years clearly means nothing to you."

The defiant side of me wanted to remind him that I *had* worked my butt off my entire life—that I was entitled to have a little fun now and then. But I knew that if I said that, we would just get into another huge argument and that was the last thing I wanted. No. The best way to show my father that I could be responsible *and* have fun, was to just do it. As my father returned to his bills, I pulled myself up and walked quietly back to my room.

Chapter Seventeen

I trudged into my room the following evening, holding my back with both hands like my grandmother does after a long car ride. Every one of my muscles ached and a shiny layer of sweat covered my entire body. My underpants and bra were soaked with it and I didn't even want to lift my arms, lest I unleash a stench strong enough to kill the cactus plant on my windowsill.

When I decided to be responsible, I was *responsible.*

I had started out my day with my usual chores down at the stable, tapping into my angry adrenaline to do them all double-time. Then I had come back to my house, cleaned all the kitchen countertops and mopped the floor and started a load of laundry. My room had been cleaned in a flash and then I had gone back down to the paddock to set up a course for me and Lola. With Penny's help, we had constructed a good array of jump heights and widths, and Lola and I had spent hours working it. We were shaky at first and, with my dad looking on, I had felt totally snagged. But we had improved quickly and by the end of our run, I was sure we would be ready for the competition in a few weeks.

By the time we were done with that, the sun was high in the sky and the humidity was thick enough to labor anyone's breathing, but I still had to help Mom and Dad with the fence. A few of the old stakes were rotted out from the spring rains and we had to dig new holes and set the new stakes in the ground. Even wearing gloves I had managed to get a nice-sized splinter in my finger and I had scraped the inside of my arm when one of the stakes slipped from my grasp. Once all that was finally done, I had to finish the mowing I had never gone back to complete after my reaming out by Marni Locke.

All in all, not a good day.

I collapsed back on my bed, too weary to

even think about the shower, and instantly, the phone rang.

I groaned and reached for the cordless on my bedside table.

"Hello?" I said, sounding drained.

"Gracie! You all right? You sound like someone died!"

I sat up at the sound of Jared's voice. "Hey! I'm so sorry I had to cancel on Pete's," I told him. When I had called him earlier to tell him I couldn't make it, he had taken it well, but I still felt awful bailing at the last minute. "Your friends must think I'm a total flake."

"I know. I told them to write you off, but for some reason, they still want to meet you," Jared joked. I heard laughter and a girl's shriek in the background. "I must have talked you up a little more than I thought."

I laughed, flushing. "Where are you?"

"We're down at the beach," he said. "Christopher and Donna and her brother are here, too. You should come down."

"Derek is there?" I asked with a rush of foreboding. How the hell had Donna convinced anti-invader Derek to hang out with them?

"Yeah, and to be honest, I don't think he likes me that much," Jared said, lowering his voice. "I think it's your turn to talk *me* up."

I bit my lip and glanced at the clock. It was five thirty. If I showered quickly I could be ready in ten minutes. Something told me that leaving Derek alone with the invaders for too long was not a good idea. And I knew Donna well enough to know that she was *not* baby-sitting her brother. Not while Christopher was around.

"Are you guys going to be there for a while?" I asked.

"Definitely," he said. "Are you sure you can come? Did you finish all your chores, Cinderella?"

"Ha ha," I said, though my stomach turned at the thought of telling my dad what I was planning to do. "I'll see you soon."

I hung up the phone, grabbed my towel and headed for the bathroom. My insides were trembling with nervous energy. As I quickly showered off all the sweat and grime, I tried to figure out how to convince my father to let me go, but then I realized how lame it all sounded. I was an adult, right? Did I really still have to ask permission to go down to the beach?

I dried off, dressed quickly and threw my hair back into a ponytail. It would have been great to get out of the house without actually having to confront my parents, but I knew by now that this tactic never worked. All it did was delay the fight. Grabbing my beach bag, I looked in the mirror and gave myself a quick pep talk. I could do this. I just had to stand up for myself.

Dad and Mom were talking in the kitchen as I made my way down the hall. That afternoon Uncle Rod had come by to let us know that surveyors had been spotted out at the Lawrence place. Apparently Mr. Kent was doing some preliminary work before the town vote even happened. Now my parents were more than ready to take their anti-Kent campaigning up a notch. Yippee. At least I was getting out of here for the night and didn't have to listen to their impassioned pleas. At least, I hoped I was.

Of course, my father took one look at me in

my bathing suit and shorts and instantly went on the offensive.

"Where do you think you're going?" he asked.

"To the beach," I said calmly. "Donna and Derek are down there with the guys and they asked me to come."

"Didn't we decide that you were staying in today?" my father asked, crossing his arms over his chest.

"Well, technically, the work day is over," I told him. "I did everything you asked me to do today, Dad. Now I'm going to go do what I want to do."

I glanced at my mother and she just gazed back at me. Was that pride I saw in her eyes? I almost smiled at the thought, but instead, I turned and crossed the room to the door. It took every ounce of strength in my tired body to get there. I kept waiting for him to say something. To yell after me and stop me from going. But he didn't. He let me go.

Huh. That wasn't so hard after all.

* * *

When I arrived at the beach, Jared was sitting in the center of a group of guys and girls, laughing and chugging a Coke. Several blankets and towels were strewn around, but the girls mostly sat in new-looking beach chairs, two of them lounging under a large umbrella. Derek was off to the side a bit, leaning back on his elbows on his towel, looking sullen. He turned around as I approached.

"Cassie!" Derek said, his face lighting up.

Jared heard him and sprang to his feet. I dropped my bag in the sand and all conversation died as everyone else looked me over curiously. Out on the lake, Donna screeched and let Christopher toss her into the water from the nearest platform. The splash was still settling as Jared gave me a big, suntan-lotiony hug and a kiss.

"Everyone, this is Cassie," he said.

They all greeted me with a round of hellos and a couple of waves. The girls seemed rather uninterested and immediately returned to their fat fashion magazines. The boys were slightly more welcoming.

"Nice to finally meet the girl Jared's been gushing about." A shortish, wiry guy with shaggy red hair stood up and offered his hand. His pale skin was burned and peeling on his shoulders. "I'm Ian."

"Hi," I replied, not sure of how to respond to the gushing comment. I shook his hand and smiled.

A couple of the other guys introduced themselves as well. The tall, chunky one was Duncan. The stocky Tom Cruise–lookalike guy was Mitch. After the introductions, Jared pointed at the girls and gave me each of their names. They all waved briefly and flashed quick, dismissive smiles. This was the type of behavior I was used to from invaders.

"Don't worry. They just don't like to be distracted from their all-important *Vogue*s," Jared whispered in my ear, grabbing my side.

I yelped and batted his hand away. "That tickled."

"Yeah, that was kind of the point," he sad with a grin.

"Hey, Cass," Derek said, getting up and

joining us. "Did you bring the truck?"

"No. I rode my bike," I told him. "Why?"

"Wanna get out of here that bad?" Jared said lightly.

Derek's eyes flashed and he looked a lot more irritated than Jared's joking comment deserved.

"What's the matter?" I asked him, lowering my voice a bit.

Derek pulled me off to the side and I cast an apologetic look over my shoulder at Jared. Maybe Derek wasn't having the best time here, but did he really need to make such a scene?

"I can't take this anymore," Derek said under his breath, glancing around. "How Donna talked me into coming here, I have no idea."

"Derek, relax," I told him. "What happened to my best friend, Mr. Fun? I thought you could have a good time anywhere."

"Yeah, not around these people," he said with a huff. "I swear all they talk about is their cars and the footage of their parents' yachts and which ski resort they're heading to for their winter breaks."

"So? They have different lives than we do,"

I said with a shrug. "Besides, I bet you could ski circles around any one of them."

"Doesn't change the fact that they look down their nose at me when I say anything," Derek replied. "Honestly, I have no idea how you and Donna can hang out with these guys. All they've done since I showed up here is judge me."

I scoffed. "I think you're being a little bit paranoid."

"And I think you're being a little bit lovesick," Derek shot back, glancing at his sister who was splashing around in the water with Christopher. "*Both* of you. That Christopher guy is such an ass. I've been watching him paw my sister all afternoon like I'm not even here."

"Ugh. I'm sorry," I said with a grimace. "But Donna likes him. What can I tell you?"

Donna laughed as she stood up in the shallow part of the water. She adjusted her bathing suit and turned to shout to Christopher, who was swimming toward her.

"Damn, Christopher hit the jackpot with that one," Duncan said to Mitch.

"I'll give the girls up here one thing," Mitch replied. "They got a lot more meat on their bones than city chicks. That girl's got plenty to grab."

My jaw dropped. Who the hell did these guys think they were?

"That's my sister you're talking about!" Derek shouted, venom spitting from his teeth.

Mitch turned around casually on the blanket and looked up at us. "Nice genes you got there, man."

No apologies. Not even a clue that he had said anything offensive. Derek stomped over to him and Mitch and Duncan both scrambled to their feet, clearly sensing that Derek was in attack mode.

"Oh, God. Not again," one of the girls grumbled, rolling her eyes.

Jared jumped between Derek and his friends and put his hands lightly on Derek's arms. "Dude, they're just being their normal idiot selves. Ignore them."

"Hey!" Duncan protested.

"Well you are, asshole," Jared shot over his shoulder, causing Duncan's face to fall. "You want to apologize or what?"

Mitch looked from Jared to Derek and

lifted one shoulder. "Sorry, man. I didn't mean anything by it," he said reluctantly.

I watched Derek's nostrils flare and his fists clench. He still wanted to fight these morons, probably because he had spent the entire afternoon listening to more idiocy like they had just spewed. Of course, the odds were definitely not in his favor, and there weren't any other locals hanging out on the beach just then to back him up in a brawl.

"Derek, come on," I said quietly. "Let it go."

He looked at me out of the corner of his eye and finally his stance relaxed. Jared dropped his hands and Derek went for his towel and wallet, grabbing Donna's keys in the process.

"Tell her I took her car," Derek said to me as he stormed right by me toward the parking lot. "Call me if either of you needs a ride."

Seconds later we all heard him peel out. The girls whispered to each other and one of them giggled. Gradually the tension in the air relaxed.

"Crisis averted," one of the girls said, lazily flipping a page in her magazine.

"You'd think the dude would like to know that his sister's a hottie," Duncan said, then laughed and slapped hands with Mitch and Ian.

Jared picked up an empty can from the ground and whipped it at Duncan's leg. "You're such a Neanderthal, man."

"Hey! Back off, Kent!" Duncan said.

But instead of making a scene this time, he simply wiped the cola dribbles off his skin with his hand and sat back down. Jared turned to me, his expression apologetic.

"You gotta excuse these guys," he said, opening his hands wide. "They don't get out much."

I smirked and tried to focus on him instead of the cretins he chose to hang out with. At least Jared had stuck up for Donna. He wasn't like his friends. And besides, they were just being guys, right? I had heard a lot worse comments during gym class at my own school. Still, I didn't exactly feel like hanging out with them just then.

"I think I'll go for a swim," I said. I unbuttoned my shorts and let them drop to the ground.

"I'm in," Jared replied.

He grabbed my hand and laced his fingers

through mine as we walked down to the water. I just hoped that the other guys weren't making comments behind *my* back now. If they liked to have stuff to grab, I could only imagine what they were saying about my scrawny self. The morons and their opinions were forgotten, however, as soon as we got to the water's edge. Donna saw me and shrieked my name as she awkwardly waded toward us through the water.

"Hey!" I called back, laughing at her level of animation. "What's going on?"

Donna threw herself into my arms and hugged me hard. Her skin was freezing cold from the water and I could feel the goose bumps on her flesh.

"Uh, maybe I'll leave you two alone." Jared took a few steps into the water, then dove head first and swam out to join Christopher.

"Guess what! Guess what! Guess what!" Donna trilled in my ear, her voice about three octaves higher than usual. "Christopher just asked me to the Summer Fling!"

My heart plummeted into my toes, but I tried to smile. Thank God Derek wasn't here for this. His worst fear had just come true.

"Really?" I croaked.

"Yeah! He likes me!" Donna said, gripping my elbows as she pulled back to look me in the eye. I hadn't seen her this excited since her dad bought her that used car of hers. "He really likes me!"

"That's . . . great," I said.

It was hard to get enthused, knowing what I knew about invaders and their expectations of local girls who were "lucky" enough to get asked to the dance. But Donna knew about that, too. We all did. Had she just completely blanked on the way history had been repeating itself for the last few summers?

"Now Jared is definitely going to ask you and all four of us can go together," Donna said, turning so that we were both facing the water.

I watched as Jared and Christopher climbed up onto the diving board platform and shoved each other around, angling for the higher board. My heart was filled with an unprecedented mixture of hope and dread. I would *love* to spend a romantic evening with Jared, all dressed up and primped and everything, so in that respect, I really wanted him to ask me. Plus we would get to hang out at the gorgeous country club all night with Donna and Christopher. At the very least, if I got to go to the dance, I could look out for Donna and the two of us would have fun together, as we always did. But if Jared *did* ask me, how would I know that he really wanted to go with me—that he wasn't expecting anything else?

If he *did* ask me, did that mean that all the time we had been spending together was a sham? Some kind of insincere game to get me to the dance and get me into bed?

For once in my life, I had no idea what to hope for.

Chapter Eighteen

For the rest of the evening, whenever the guys weren't around, all Donna could talk about was the dance. She was positive Jared was going to ask me and she kept making herself scarce whenever he was nearby, just to give him the chance. The whole song and dance got me all worked up to the point that I spent the next couple of hours half-tense, waiting for him to drop the bomb and trying to figure out what I would say.

But he never did. And somehow, that made me even more tense. His best friend was going with my best friend. Why hadn't he asked me? I mean, I wasn't positive that I wanted to go, but it might be nice to be *asked*. Unless, of course, he really *did* just want sex.

Suffice it to say, I was really confused.

But by the next morning, after waiting for the phone to ring half the night, I was nothing but irritated. Why hadn't he asked me to the dance? We were dating. What was he going to do, invite some private school girl up from the Hamptons to accompany him? Was I not good enough for his precious country club?

I took my frustration out on the horses the next morning, brushing them vigorously and muttering the entire time. I'm pretty sure Lola thought I was losing it. She didn't even try to nuzzle me once. My vibe was probably freaking her out.

Still, I took her out and practiced jumping for a while in the late morning. It was a cloudy, muggy day, which did nothing to help my mood. By the time we were done with our exercises, we were both panting. I led her back to the stable, gave her some water in her bucket, and dropped down on the bench against the outside wall with my own bottle. I sucked half of it down without a breath, feeling much better.

Then Jared's car turned into the driveway. When I saw it, I wasn't sure *what* to feel. Hopeful?

Annoyed? What? Music blared through the windows as he pulled to a stop in front of the stable, and the moment I saw him, annoyance won out. I guess that was my defense mechanism kicking in.

"Hey good lookin'," he said jokingly, leaning over the passenger seat. "Wanna go for a ride?"

Unbelievable. I felt my blood boiling just below the surface. How could he be so casual when I was internally freaking out over here?

"No. Not really," I said coolly. I took Lola's reins and led her back inside the stable.

"Hey!" Jared called out.

I heard the engine die, killing the music, and the door slam. He followed me inside and stood back while I put Lola in her stall. I could feel his eyes boring into my back and I wished he would just go away. At that moment I had no idea what I wanted from him and that feeling was even more frustrating with him standing right there looking all gorgeous.

"Hey, what's the matter?" he asked.

"Nothing," I replied. I turned around and shrugged. "Nothing at all."

"You're mad," Jared said. "What did I do?

Is it about Derek yesterday? Because I called over there last night to apologize again. He seemed pretty cool about it, so—"

"Oh, you called *there* last night, huh?" I said, talking before I could think.

Jared blinked. His brows knit. "I'm sorry. Was I supposed to call *you*? Is that what this is about? If I was, I'm sorry. I just—"

"No. That's not it. Forget it," I said, turning my back on him.

I walked into the tack room, grabbed a saddle at random, and threw it down on the table. Maybe a little buffing would help work out my aggression. Jared appeared in the doorway and leaned casually against the side. He looked at me in this sort of condescending way that did nothing for my internal thermometer. Couldn't he just take a hint and go away already?

"This is about the dance, isn't it?" he said.

"No," I lied.

"Yes it is. Christopher asked Donna and now you want me to ask you," he said.

Oh. My. God. Could he *be* any more egotistical?

"Well, just so you know, that's why I came

over here," he said, walking around the table until he was only inches away. "So what do you say? Want to go to the Summer Fling?"

My pulse raced with excitement and I tried not to smile. Instead, I went against every impulse in my body, looked him square in the eye and said, "No."

It was worth just the expression of total bafflement on his face. "What?"

"Thanks for asking, though," I said.

"Is this because I didn't ask you yesterday?" he demanded. "I didn't want to do it in front of all those people. That's the only reason."

"Look, it's not a big deal," I said, dropping the leather brush and turning to him. "I just don't want to go."

"Why not?" Jared asked, clearly offended.

"Because!" I gave him a meaningful look and he just stared at me blankly. "You an invader . . . me a local . . . God! Are you really going to make me say it?"

"Apparently," Jared said, crossing his arms over his chest. "'Cuz I have no idea what you're talking about."

I sighed and my shoulders slumped. "Look,

everyone in this town knows why invaders ask local girls to the dance. It's a long-standing tradition, okay? And I'm not that kind of girl."

Realization dawned on Jared's face, followed quickly by total amusement. "Come on! Do you really think that's why I'm asking you?"

My face burned. "Well, I don't know. History has a way of repeating itself, right?"

"Gracie!" he said, his eyes dancing. He slipped his arms around me and I didn't resist. "That is not what this is about," he said, looking me in the eye and growing serious. "Come on. You know how I feel about you."

My heart pounded so hard I could feel it from my fingertips to my toes. "I do?"

"Please! I don't show my landfill of a room to just anyone," he said. "And I've never let anybody drive my car—not even my mom. You've seen me at my drunken worst and you still, for some reason, seem to want to hang out with me."

I smiled and looked down at the place where my T-shirt met with his. He touched his forehead to mine and I looked up. His eyes were staring directly into mine.

"You're all I think about, Gracie," he said.

"All the time. I've never felt this way about anyone. I think . . . I think I'm falling in love with you."

I would have collapsed if he hadn't been holding me. My heart felt like it exploded into a thousand tiny pieces. I was overwhelmed with happiness and completely floored.

I love you, too, I thought, giddy. *I love you, I love you, I love you.*

But I didn't say anything. I couldn't. I had only just been kissed for the first time. How did I know if I was in love? Reliable, predictable, responsible Cassie took over and kept my tongue firmly rooted to the bottom of my mouth.

Jared looked at me intently. I had to say something. Anything. But before I could he pressed his lips to mine and kissed me softly. Excitement rushed through me and I felt like I was at war with myself. Part of me wanted to cling to him and tell him I loved him back. But another part of me—a big part—knew that he was leaving in a few weeks and that I would have to be an idiot to get in deeper than I already was.

When we finally broke apart, I was shaking and confused tears stung at my eyes. I threw my arms around his neck and hugged him so hard he groaned. I had to get a grip.

"Okay! You don't have to strangle me!" he said, pushing me gently away. "So will you go to the dance with me or what?"

Thank God he wasn't pressing the "love" issue. I knew when I had dodged a serious bullet.

"Oh, I am *so* there," I told him, laughing with relief.

My glee was short-lived, however. I heard another car pull into the drive and stood on my tiptoes to see out the high tack room window. Marni Locke's SUV was pulling up at an indecent speed.

"What is *she* doing here?" I said with a moan. "Come to ream me out again?"

"Is this the be-yotch?" Jared asked, checking the window as I stepped away.

"Oh, yeah."

I sighed and walked out to the large stable door. Mrs. Locke parked over by the fence, got out, and started wrangling her two kids out of the car.

"What the . . . ? We don't have a lesson today," I told Jared.

"Cassandra!" Mrs. Locke called out, waving at me. "I need you to take the kids!"

My jaw hit the dirt. "Oh no way," I muttered. "What does she think I am, a baby-sitter?"

Little Josh was shrieking and pulling at his mother's hand as she tried to drag him toward me. Seth was already climbing the fence around the paddock, something I had told him ten million times not to do.

"You have to tell this woman off," Jared said in my ear. "You can do it, Gracie. Just tell her you're not at her beck and call."

He turned around and pretended to be fascinated by the horses' pedigrees, which hung on the wall near the door. Marni shot him a curious look, but quickly turned her attention to me. Her hair was slicked back in such a tight bun it was pulling her eyes into slits.

"I need you to give the boys an extra lesson," she said, trying to detach Josh, who was now crying himself red, from her arm. "I'm going shopping. I'll be back in an hour."

"I—"

"Make sure you don't let them get dirty this time," she said flatly. "I do not have time to give them another bath tonight."

My pulse raced with anger and humiliation. *Say something, Cassie. She can't get away with this.*

Jared shot me a look over her shoulder, widening his eyes and pursing his lips. *"Do it!"* he mouthed. *"Come on! You can do it!"*

She finally managed to fling Josh away and he turned around and clung to the wall instead, looking up at her with sad eyes. "Be good!" she told him. Then she turned on her heel and stalked off.

"Gracie," Jared hissed.

"Wait!" I shouted.

I bent down and picked Josh up. He was all hot and wet and he grasped my shirt with his little fists.

"I'm sorry, Mrs. Locke, but I can't take care of your children for you," I said, my heart pounding in my ears.

She clucked her tongue. "I *really* don't have time for this."

"No, *I* don't have time for this," I said. "This is not our normal lesson period. Now, if you want to schedule extra lessons, you can call my father and set up a time and payment schedule. But for now, I'm gonna have to ask you to take your kids and go."

I tilted Josh toward her and he reached out for her with both arms. She had to grab him or he was going to topple right over. The moment he was back with his mother, he curled up against her chest.

"I'm going to *pay* you," she said, frustrated.

"But as I said, I am not available right now," I told her, hoping I wasn't visibly trembling. "I'm not your on-call baby-sitter, Mrs. Locke. I'm a riding instructor. I will continue to give the boys lessons at their scheduled time, but that's it."

Her mouth hung open as she gaped at me. Clearly this was not going the way she had planned.

"Oh, and I think Josh there has a fever," I

told her. "You might want to take him to the doctor in town."

Mrs. Locke felt Josh's head quickly, then rolled her eyes. "Seth! Let's go!" she shouted.

Seth, maybe sensing the panic and irritation in his mother's voice, dropped right to the ground and ran for the car. Mrs. Locke buckled her kids in and shot me one last, annoyed look before peeling out. The moment she was gone, I turned around and squealed with glee.

"I did it!"

"You were awesome!" Jared cheered.

I was quaking all over, unable to believe that I had actually just stood up to an adult. That I had held my own with Marni Locke of all people. I don't know if it was adrenaline or glee or me just trying to work out my confusion over Jared, but I had done it. I was as light as air as Jared kissed me hard and hugged me off my feet. In my whole life, I had never felt so free.

Chapter Nineteen

I loved my prom dress. I loved my prom dress so much, in fact, that I had found the Lake Logan High School Senior Prom to be unworthy of it. How could it not have been? It was a high school dance with a bad DJ held in the same gym we had sweat it out in for four years under crepe paper streamers and a disco ball missing a third of its mirrors. Plus, Donna and I had gone dateless, figuring it would be more fun to hang out with each other than pair up with any of the slim pickin's our school had to offer. We were right, of course. We had a fabulous time and didn't have to worry about whether or not some dork was going to try to kiss us at the end of the night. So it had turned out okay.

But the Lake Logan Country Club Summer

Fling—that was a whole different story.

I twirled in front of the mirror that night, admiring the way my aqua blue skirt fluttered and fell around my ankles. My dress had a halter top and an asymmetrical hem and made me feel like I could actually be photographed for one of Donna's many celebrity rags. My hair was back in a bun, but I had let some tendrils fall around my face. I was tan and flushed and giddy with anticipation. This night blew prom out of the water, and it hadn't even started yet.

"Cassie! He's here!" my mom called out.

My heart went into overdrive and I quickly fixed my hair and applied a little more lip gloss. I could hear the car tires crunching on the driveway as I grabbed my little silver bag. I had to laugh at the eager, kid-on-Christmas-morning expression on my own face.

"Okay, chill," I told myself. "It's just a dance."

But it didn't feel like "just" anything.

I walked out to the living room where my mother and father were waiting for me, camera at the ready. My father smiled and stood up from the couch when he saw me.

"You look beautiful, Cassie," he said proudly.

I grinned. "Thanks, Dad."

I was touched that he had put aside all of his irritation toward the Kents for one night. In fact, my parents seemed to be pleasantly surprised when I had told them about the dance. Apparently they thought that it meant that Jared was serious about me and not just messing with my head. I guess my parents hadn't heard all the rumors about what invaders and local girls really did at these things. Thank the Lord. Otherwise, I would be locked in my room right now and Dad would be outside with the shotgun.

My mother snapped a picture of me just as the doorbell rang. My heart was bumping around inside of me like a hummingbird. Dad opened the door and greeted Jared with a firm handshake and a manly nod.

"Mr. Grace," Jared said.

"Jared," my father replied. "Good to see you."

Thank you, Dad! Thank you, thank you, thank you!

When Jared stepped inside a moment later, I truly felt as if time had stopped. Jared in a T-shirt was hot. Jared in a tuxedo, however, was *come-to-mama*. His hair was tousled just perfectly and his blue eyes looked piercing as he smiled from across the room. He held a plastic box with a flower inside. My very first corsage! We shared a quick glance, and then he greeted my mother.

"You must be Mrs. Grace," he said, offering his hand. "It's a pleasure to meet you."

My mother, I swear, actually blushed. How could you not with a gorgeous specimen like that touching your hand?

"Gracie," Jared said, crossing over to me. "You look incredible."

My grin, if possible, widened. "So do you."

He opened the box and pulled out a single white orchid on an elastic band. "For you," he said, with a little bow of his head.

"It's beautiful," I told him, holding out my hand.

Jared slid the flower into place and then squeezed my hand. Shivers ran all up and down my arm. Oh yeah, he was a far superior date to Donna.

"Shall we get a picture?" my mother asked.

"Can I suggest that we go outside?" Jared said. "Your lovely ranch would make an incredible backdrop."

Man, was he laying it on thick.

Mom, however, was eating it up. "Of course. Good idea," she said. She smiled, flattered, and led the way to the door.

Jared and I stood together on the front walk, the fields and the mountains behind us, and lightly draped our arms around each other. My father handled it all very well, keeping his mouth shut and only clearing his throat a couple of times. As my mother snapped away, I realized that at that moment, I couldn't have been happier. I was posing for pictures with an amazing guy in a gorgeous dress. My parents were actually getting along with him. And I had a whole night of surprises ahead of me. I could hardly wait to get started.

"So this is the Lake Logan Country Club," Donna said, wrapping her arm around mine as we entered the Gold Ballroom. "Not bad."

"Wait 'til you see the Platinum Ballroom," I joked. "This isn't even their best room."

The boys trailed behind us as we walked around the periphery of the smaller of the club's two ballrooms, gazing out the floor-to-ceiling windows that looked out over the pond at the center of the golf course. Little candles in white bags had been set up all around the water, their light reflected in the rippling surface. White Chinese lanterns draped from the trees, bouncing slightly in the breeze. Someone around here was doing their homework when it came to ambience. It was like looking out at a fairyland.

Donna sighed luxuriously. "I always wondered how the other half lived."

"Yeah. Funny how so many real Lake Loganers have never stepped foot inside the Lake Logan Country Club," I whispered, earning a stifled giggle.

I was so glad that Donna and I were here together. Without her presence I would have been a lot more nervous than I already was.

Before the dance, a formal dinner was being held for the guests. Long tables dotted the room, covered in crisp white tablecloths and set with pristine white china plates, each of which had a swirling gold "LLCC" in the center. Tapered candles flickered down the center of each table and the lights were dimmed low, giving the room a sleepy feel. But the anticipation of the dance was still there, charging the room with a certain energy.

We took our assigned seats near the center of our table, I was disappointed to see that Donna and Christopher were sitting all the way at the far end. A waiter came over and laid my napkin in my lap for me before handing me a menu. I smiled and thanked him. No one had ever laid my napkin in my lap for me before.

"What's good here?" I asked Jared.

"Pretty much everything," he replied.

But I barely heard him. His parents had just been ushered to their seats directly across from us. Jared had already introduced us outside, but I had been hoping that I wouldn't have to spend the whole night with their appraising eyes watching me. Bad luck, however. It looked as if the country club gods had decided to sit all the families together. Christopher's parents, his younger brother, and his date were all slipping into chairs around Donna and Chris as well.

This was going to be interesting.

The waiter circled our table, taking entrée orders. It seemed every woman there was on a diet, as they all ordered grilled salmon or the vegetable plate. Jared's father leaned back in his seat and loudly ordered the filet mignon, extra rare. I felt Jared stiffen next to me and glanced at him, wondering what was wrong. He wouldn't meet my eye, and instead stared down at the elaborate menu like it held the meaning of life.

"Nothing I love better than a red piece of meat," he said, patting his stomach as the men around him laughed,

Jared's mother stoically turned away from him and sipped her water.

"For you, miss?" the waiter asked when he reached my chair.

"I'll have the filet mignon please," I told him. "Medium."

"And I'll have the swordfish," Jared said.

Then he flicked his finger at the waiter, who leaned toward him. "Bring my father the grilled salmon," he said.

"But sir, he ordered the steak," the waiter replied, flustered.

"I know," Jared said. "There's a fifty in it for you if you bring him the salmon. Trust me, he won't make a scene."

He pulled a crisp folded bill out of his pocket and slipped it to the waiter surreptitiously. The waiter nodded slightly and moved on. I wasn't sure whether to feel impressed or appalled that he was undermining his dad and bribing a waiter. Either way, I was confused.

"What was that all about?" I whispered.

"That was about my father not knowing what's good for him," Jared answered without looking at me. Then he turned to the guy on his left and struck up a conversation. Clearly, the subject was closed.

The girl to my right, whose name was Eve, was talking to her other neighbor, leaving me to stare at my water glass in silence. I glanced down the table at Donna and Christopher who seemed to be having a grand old time, gabbing away. I wished I was down there with them instead of feeling conspicuous, sitting there with no one to talk to. But soon Jared returned his attention to me, and the tension he had been oozing seconds before was gone.

All through the appetizers I sat in my chair at attention, my back straight and my elbows pinned to my sides to keep from leaning them on the table. Whatever their past reputation, tonight I wanted to make a good impression on Jared's parents.

Donna, on the other hand, was laughing it up with Christopher and his family at the far end of the table, swigging from her water glass and resting her arm on the back of Christopher's chair. I envied her ability to be so relaxed.

My filet mignon was placed in front of me and Eve leaned toward my ear.

"You ordered the steak?" she said in awe, her flowery perfume filling my nostrils. "Brave girl. Where *do* you put it all?"

Her shrewd brown eyes flicked over my body and she smiled tightly. I looked at her plate—steamed fish, steamed vegetables—and tried not to grimace. She was already nothing but skin and bones. I guess this was the type of city girl Duncan and Mitch had been talking about when they were admiring Donna's bod.

"I like a girl who knows how to eat," Jared said lightly, slicing into his fish.

Eve sniffed and cut a tiny piece of a carrot stalk. She chewed it for about ten minutes.

I stiffened as Jared's father received his meal, wondering how he was going to react. He registered surprise, but before he could say anything, Jared's mother loudly struck up a conversation. With me.

"So, Cassandra, it's so nice to finally meet you," she said, addressing me for the first time since we had been introduced. She had turned out to be a beautiful woman, a bit on the plump side, with thick blond hair and blue eyes that matched Jared's perfectly, except that they were dull and apprising instead of sharp and sparkling. She wore a black strapless gown and her neck and fingers dripped with more rocks than we had in the mountains surrounding Lake Logan. "How has your mother been?" she asked. "We used to be such good friends."

Prickly heat rushed up my neck and into

my face at the casual mention of my mother and their friendship. My mom was still heartbroken about what happened — so much so that she had never even talked about it until this summer. But here was Mrs. Kent, throwing it out there like it was nothing.

Meanwhile, Jared's dad was cutting into his fish without a word. No one else at the table seemed to realize he had received the wrong meal, even after his loud declaration of love for red meat. So weird. Was this just some kind of odd game Jared and his family played?

"Really?" Jared said, raising his eyebrows. "I never knew that."

"Yeah. They went to high school together," I said, trying to match Mrs. Kent's light tone.

And then your mother stabbed my mother in the back, ran off with your dad, and never spoke to my mom again, I added silently.

Mr. Kent laughed at something the man next to him said and I felt a sudden rush of guilt. What was I doing here chatting with these people? They had caused my mother so much misery and now they were trying to buy off my town. They were the worst of the worst when it came to invaders, and I was sitting at their club sipping champagne with them.

"So is she well?" Mrs. Kent asked me, her diamond rings sparkling in the candlelight as she reached for her glass.

"Very well, thanks," I managed to say.

"That's good to hear," she replied. Then she moved on to a conversation with the woman on her left. Half of me was irritated that she didn't seem interested in hearing more. The other half was relieved that I didn't have to keep talking to her.

I sighed and turned to Jared. "How long is the dinner part of this thing?"

"Probably about another hour," he said. "There'll be dessert and coffee and then we'll move into the Platinum room for the dance. Why? Are you completely bored?"

"Oh, no! I'm fine!" I said with a bright smile.

"You're a bad liar. But thanks for trying," he replied. "We'll bail as soon as we can."

My smile widened. "Thanks."

"Well *I* still can't believe that the Westons bought a house in Long Beach, of all places," the woman sitting next to Mrs. Kent said.

"A travesty," another lady put in.

"I told him that an estate half the size in Sag Harbor would benefit him much more than that monstrosity he bought, but who listens to me anymore?" Mr. Kent joked, earning a round of hearty laughs from the men at the table.

"Next he's going to be moving his family to Soho," the first woman joked.

"What's wrong with Soho?" I whispered to Jared, taking a small bite of my steak.

"Nothing. They're just being snobs," Jared replied. "Ignore them."

I smirked and returned to my meal. Two girls across the table were discussing the recent sample sales in the city, while a pair of boys argued over which of the new ski lines were better than the others. Meanwhile, the parents continued their assessment of the properties held by people who weren't there to defend their lifestyle choices.

I looked at Jared and he rolled his eyes. I hid a laugh behind my water glass. That was when I remembered I wasn't here to chat with the insufferable people at the table. I was here for him. And that was more than enough.

"How incredible is this?" Donna asked, dropping into a chair a few hours later, all out of breath from dancing.

I fell into the seat next to her and kicked off my shoes. My feet throbbed in thanks. "Pretty incredible," I responded with a grin.

The tables were set up outside on the stone patio where waiters circulated, taking drink orders from those who needed a breather from the action inside. Three sets of double glass doors had been thrown open and on the other side, hundreds of guests in designer duds got down on the circular dance floor. Every last one of them was trying to look natural as they jerked around to the band's rendition of the latest dance hit. Few succeeded, but everyone was having fun. Huge flower pots lined the walls inside, bursting with gorgeous lilies and roses.

It was an amazing scene. Best of all, none of us had seen any of the parents since dinner had ended. It was as if they had disappeared to some secret place in the club and left the real partying to the younger set. That meant I could wriggle my bare toes and stretch out on the patio with no fear of Jared's parents seeing and judging.

"You and Christopher were getting a little hot and heavy out there, huh?" I said.

"Omigosh, he is so hot, Cass," Donna said. "It is definitely not fair that we grew up with the dorks we grew up with when there were guys like him running around out there."

I grinned. "I'm glad you like him so much."

"I do," she said, tapping her foot. I could tell she was already getting antsy to rejoin him and his friends on the dance floor.

"And?" I said.

"And what?"

"And how does he feel about you?" I asked her.

She smirked. "Well, he hasn't said he *loves* me like *some* people," Donna said, rolling her eyes and laughing. "But he likes me, too. He's such a good guy. It's too bad he's only up here for the summer."

My heart felt full as I watched Jared chatting with his friends inside. "I know what you mean."

I was relieved to see that Donna was so happy and so confident that Christopher really liked her. Clearly I had nothing to worry about. It seemed like we had found the only two worthwhile invaders out there.

"So, have you said it back yet?" Donna asked.

I sighed. "No. And thankfully he hasn't said it again."

"You are one insane woman," Donna said, shaking her head.

"I know," I said with a groan. "Why can't I just tell him? I mean, how do you actually know?"

"I think you're just supposed to know," Donna replied. "But you do, trust me."

"Pardon?"

"I can tell. You should see the way you are around him. You're like a whole different Cassie. I mean, in a good way," Donna said. "You love him, you're just too much of a repressed freak to say it."

I laughed. "Gee, thanks."

"Don't worry. You'll get up the guts," she told me, narrowing her eyes. "You've been doing a lot of things differently this summer. I know you'll figure it out."

I smiled and felt the knot in my chest loosen a bit. "You're good to have around, D."

"I know," she said blithely.

Jared broke away from his friends and strolled over to join us. He held out his hand just as a slow song started up inside. My heart pounded like mad as he smiled languidly.

"May I have this dance?" he asked.

"Do I have to wear my shoes?" I replied.

"You don't have to wear anything you don't want to wear," Jared joked.

"Ooh. Kinky," Donna said.

I laughed and took Jared's hand, letting him lead me back inside. Donna got up and followed us, quickly finding Christopher hovering on the side of the dance floor. I slipped my arms around Jared's neck and he held me close, swaying lazily to the music.

"So, are you having a good time?" he asked, his voice all husky. I could feel the reverberations through his chest and into my arms.

"The best time," I replied.

"Me, too," he said.

"Jared, can I ask you a question?" I said, still burning with curiosity over what happened at dinner.

"Anything."

"What was up with you bribing the waiter tonight?" I asked him. "Do you always order for your dad?"

Jared took a deep breath and looked past my shoulder. "I don't really feel like talking about my parents," he said lightly.

My heart thumped extra hard and I tried not to look too thrown, but it was difficult. Why was Jared always ducking my questions? He said I could ask him anything, but then he refused to answer. Didn't he want to be close with me?

"But I—"

"Come on, Gracie," he said with that heart-stopping smile of his. He held me a little closer and my pulse raced. "For one night, let's pretend that there's just us. You and me. No one else in the world exists."

I felt tingly all over and smiled. Okay, so I was sucked in by a little romance. I could hardly blame myself. Up until this summer, my life had been romance-free. And Jared was really, *really* good at it.

"Okay, fine," I said, my heart feeling light. "Just for tonight."

"Good. Because there's something I've been wanting to do ever since I first saw you in that dress," he said.

"What's that?" I asked, breathless.

"Just this," he replied.

Then he leaned down and kissed me so slowly and tenderly everything inside of me melted, including my mind and any questions that were still buzzing around inside of it. I rested the weight of my body against him as I floated somewhere up near the vaulted ceiling. I was no longer worried about whether or not Jared wanted us to be close. This was definitely close enough for me.

Chapter Twenty

Jared and I spent the next hour walking around the pond, stumbling upon couples kissing in the grass, and stealing kisses for ourselves. We finally found a relatively quiet spot on the far side of one of the Chinese lantern trees. Jared laid out his tuxedo jacket for me and we sat down and cuddled up together, unable to stop touching each other for even a second. I have no idea how long we were there, kissing, talking, and kissing some more, but by the time we decided to finally tear ourselves away, I felt loopy and giggly and warm.

Maybe I *was* in love.

"Want to go back inside?" Jared asked, looking out across the grounds to the ballroom, where the band was currently kicking it up a notch. The strains of guitar and the pounding of the drums carried across the water and someone's shout was chorused by dozens of responding hollers.

His jacket was draped around my shoulders now and I held it closer to me. I felt like if we went back in there and partied, I would lose the cozy, happy vibe I was working just then, and I didn't want that to happen.

"Actually . . ." I said, not wanting to disappoint him.

"Yeah, I know what you mean," he said, taking my hand. "Let's get out of here."

We strolled over to the parking lot and were about to make our way up to the valet stand, when I saw a flash of red out of the corner of my eye. I turned and suddenly the balloon that had been floating me along for the past couple of hours completely deflated.

It was Donna. She was leaning back against the rear bumper of Jared's car, her hair a ragged mess and her eye makeup smudged from crying. There was a scrape on her left knee. The moment she saw me, she stood up and her lip started to quiver.

"Oh my God," I said under my breath.

"Donna?" Jared said.

I don't even remember how I got to her. The next second I was hugging her tight and she was sobbing all over my shoulder.

"Are you okay?" I asked her over and over again. "Donna? Are you okay? What happened?"

Donna cast a look at Jared and wiped under her eyes. I was trembling with the suspicion of what might have happened when I looked over at him, my mouth set in a tight line.

"Could you give us a second?" I asked.

Jared's skin was pale and waxy. He nodded without a word and turned away, walking a few car spaces down the row to give us a little privacy.

"Was it Christopher?" I asked Donna, still holding onto her arms.

She nodded and the tears started anew. "I feel like such an ass. I really thought he liked me."

I felt as if someone was tearing my heart with an X-Acto knife. "What did he do?"

"Nothing," she said, sniffling. "I mean, we

went out to the pool house and I just thought we were gonna fool around a little, you know? But then he whips out this condom and I'm like, 'Not gonna happen.' And then he basically flipped out and broke up with me."

I know it sounds awful, but I felt relieved. "He didn't hurt you?" I asked. "How did you get that scrape?"

Donna snorted and wrapped her arms around herself. "I was crying and I couldn't see where I was going and I tripped."

"He left you out there alone?" I asked, my stomach turning.

"Yeah, well. Guess that's what you get for being a 'tease,'" she said, adding some air quotes. She laughed shortly, then burst into tears all over again. I hugged her hard, wishing Christopher were there right now so I could strangle him. How could he string Donna along like that? How could he make her think he liked her when all he was interested in was sex?

"That's it," Jared blurted, just behind me. I hadn't even realized that he had gravitated back toward us while Donna was talking.

"Jared—"

"No. He's such an asshole," Jared said, his face growing red. "I can't believe I hooked you up with him Donna, I am so, *so* sorry."

"It's okay," she said weepily. "It's not your fault."

"No, it's not. It's his," he said. "It's his fault for being such a loser."

He turned on his heel and started back toward the country club, pushing up the sleeves of his shirt.

"Jared? Where are you going?" I shouted.

"Guess!" Jared snapped.

"Don't!" Donna cried, scurrying after him. "You don't have to do this."

I grabbed her purse and mine and hurried in their wake.

"Yes. I do," he replied.

"Jared, come on," I begged. "Do you really want to start a fight with your best friend right now? Maybe we should all go home and cool down and deal with this tomorrow."

"Not an option," Jared said.

He reached the outer door to the Platinum room and stormed right through. The music was deafening after the quiet of the golf course.

Christopher was hamming it up right in the middle of the dance floor, grinding with Eve in her skimpy black dress. The crowd around him noticed the ire in Jared's expression and parted to let him through, each of them probably hoping that he wasn't out for *their* blood.

"You!" Jared shouted at the top of his lungs.

Christopher whirled around, grinning doofily, and was met with a serious right hook to the jaw. The crack was loud enough that everyone on the dance floor stopped instantly. The music slowly ground to a halt. Christopher went down and the girls around me gasped. For a split second no one moved. Jared's labored breathing was the only sound marring the silence.

"What the hell was that for?" Christopher asked, holding his jaw and glaring up at Jared from the floor.

"For playing right into the stereotype, jackass," Jared said.

Then he turned around and looked at Donna. "Come on," he said, lightly draping his arm over her shoulders and turning her around. "I'll take you home."

* * *

My good-night kiss with Jared was not quite as romantic as I had hoped. We stood outside Donna's house under the Policastros' porch light, feeling grim.

"You sure you don't want me to take you home?" he asked, his hands in his pockets.

"No, thanks. I'm gonna stay with her tonight," I said. "But thank you for driving us here. You were great tonight."

Jared scoffed and looked past my shoulder into the darkness. "Yeah. Right."

"You were," I said, reaching out and tugging on his lapel. "You defended my best friend's honor. What's more romantic than that?"

He smirked in a self-deprecating way and looked down at me. "Not getting her into a situation in which her honor has to be defended?" he suggested.

I smiled. "You're sweet, but it's not your fault Christopher's a pig." A cool breeze kicked up and I rubbed my bare arms. Was it really just an hour ago that Jared and I were all cuddled up and warm and happy beside that big old tree? "You should go. I have to get back inside."

"Okay," Jared said reluctantly. "I'll call you tomorrow."

He squeezed my arm and gave me a peck on the cheek. My big, romantic night had officially come to an end.

But I wasn't thinking about myself for long. Donna was the girl I was worried about. Fifteen minutes later we sat in the center of her bed with an open pint of Ben & Jerry's Phish Food in front of us. I was wearing borrowed pj's and Donna was all cleaned up and sporting her favorite Indiana University sweatshirt. That was Donna—always looking ahead when everyone else would probably be obsessively looking back.

"All I can say is, thank God Derek wasn't up when we got home," Donna said. "We would have had a murder on our hands."

"You're not gonna tell him?" I asked.

"Please," Donna said with a snort. "I never wanted to be an only child."

I grinned. "You've wanted to be an only child every day of your life."

"Yeah, well. You know what I mean," she replied.

"I'm so sorry this happened, Donna," I said. "But I'm glad you weren't hurt."

"Like that wuss could hurt me? Please," she said, shaking her hair back. "We saw a garter snake in the woods that day by the lake and I swear he squealed like a girl."

I laughed. "You're taking this well."

"Talk to me in three days when I've got Avril on permanent repeat and I'm still wearing these clothes," she said.

We dug into the ice cream in silence for a while, my mind filled with the events of the night. In was unreal how five hours of amazing could be completely obliterated by ten minutes of horror.

"You know, I'm starting to think we had it wrong all along," Donna said quietly. "Maybe Lake Logan guys *are* the cream of the crop."

"Bite your tongue," I replied.

"Hey, you never know until you try," Donna said, sliding her legs under her comforter and leaning back against her pillows. I lifted the carton of ice cream so she could stretch out. "I, for one, will be steering clear of invaders from here on out."

I swallowed against a lump in my throat. "All of them?" I asked, pretending I was mesmerized by the dregs of the ice cream.

"Well, not Jared of course," she said, knowing exactly what I was asking. "I really think you found a good one, there."

"You do?" I asked. After all, earlier that night I had thought we'd found *two* good ones. Doesn't say much for my judgment.

"Well, he laid out Christopher," she joked. "That gets some points in my book."

I laughed lightly and tossed the carton into the garbage can.

"Seriously, though, Cass," she said wearily. "Jared is good people. Invader or no invader. Kent or no Kent." She paused and sighed. "You lucky stiff."

I smiled at her sadly and reached for the light. "Come on. Let's get some sleep."

"Thanks, Cassie," she said, as we were doused in darkness. "I'm sorry if I ruined your night."

"Please. Who else would I want to end the most romantic evening of my life with, but you?" I teased.

"Ha ha," she said flatly.

I gave her a quick kiss on the cheek and dropped down on the floor, shoving my feet into the sleeping bag I had slept in so many times before. I fluffed up the pillow and laid down on my back, staring up at the ceiling and the faded poster of Justin Timberlake that Donna had taped there about ten years ago.

"I really thought he liked me," Donna said quietly.

The loneliness in her voice nearly ripped my heart out. "I know, D. But he was so not worthy."

"G'night," she said.

"Good night," I replied.

Pretty soon Donna, who could fall asleep in the middle of a rodeo, was breathing heavily, but I was as alert as could be. Maybe Jared was, in fact, good people, but that didn't mean I hadn't gotten in too deep with him. Until tonight I had never met his family, I knew nothing about his world. His friends I *had* met, but clearly I knew nothing about them, either. Yet here I was, shirking my lessons, straining my relationship with my parents and with Derek, and for what?

A picture of Jared's gorgeous face appeared in my mind's eye and I tried my best to wipe it away. When it came right down to it, Jared was still an invader. He was only here for the summer. It was going to have to end sooner rather than later—maybe not as messily as Donna's relationship had ended, but still. I had turned my life upside down to hang out with a guy who was only temporary. I hadn't accomplished any of the goals I had set out for myself last spring. Not one. And my goals had always been my life.

I rolled over onto my side as if that could quiet my confused heart. Donna was going to be steering clear of the invaders from now on, and maybe I should too, for a while. Concentrate on what I needed to do. Get my priorities in order.

Keep myself from ending up like Donna.

Chapter Twenty-one

*F*or the next few days I was all about my chores. I may have done more work on the ranch than I had the entire rest of my life put together. I raked, I mowed, I seeded, I swept, I mended, I painted, I scrubbed. Every day my muscles ached and I started going to bed earlier and earlier, passing out one night on top of my covers, my denim shorts and tank top still clinging to my dirt-caked skin.

At lessons, I was Miss No-Nonsense. Not that I had ever been very loosey-goosey in the past, but now I tolerated no mistakes. I made Shelby practice a fence jump about twenty-five times in a row until she finally got it right. My first-year students progressed through three lessons of work in one hour. Even the Locke boys seemed to recognize my new attitude. They only tried to make each other eat dirt once.

All this in an attempt to keep my mind off of Jared. He called a couple of times and listening to his messages made my heart ache, but I deleted each one. I needed time to figure out what I wanted to do, and I had a feeling that if I saw him, I wasn't going to be able to think clearly.

What I needed was fresh air and hard work to free my mind. And was I ever getting a lot of it.

As I walked into the house that evening, my dad was just hanging up the phone. I heard him swear under his breath and my heart thumped.

"Dad?" I said, coming into the kitchen.

He looked up at me and sighed. "That was Jim Policastro," he said. "They decided to take Robert Kent up on his offer."

I felt like my insides had frozen. I knew this was exactly what Donna wanted—and exactly the news my father had been praying not to hear.

"What are you going to do?" I asked.

"Well, we can still stop the development," my father said, crossing to the kitchen table, where some notes were laid out. "Just because he made a deal with Jim doesn't mean he made a deal with the rest of us. His plans still have to get past the town planning board. If we make a good argument, we can head him off there."

"So . . . you're not mad at Donna and Derek's parents, right?" I asked.

"No, Cassie," he said with a sigh. "Disappointed, but not mad. I know how much they love that old place. And they have to look out for their family."

I let out a relieved breath and trudged over to the refrigerator. At least I wouldn't have to deal with my father's coldness over another one of my friends.

"Long day?" he asked me.

"You could say that," I replied. "Got a good workout with Lola, though. We're definitely going to be ready for the competition."

If I have enough cash to enter, I added silently. As it stood, my old jelly jar that I had set aside for the championship fund was only about half as full as it should have been.

"That's what I like to hear," my father told me. "You've been working really hard lately,

Cassie. I'm glad to see you've come around."

Why did he have to put it that way? It just made my toes curl. But there was no energy in me to pick a fight. And besides, part of me knew he was right all along.

"Thanks," I said flatly.

I took my apple juice and headed back to my room to grab my shower stuff. As soon as I closed the door behind me, the phone rang. My heart slammed around in my chest, but I let it ring. I knew it might be Jared, and I wasn't sure what I wanted to say to him yet.

Actually, that was something I had been avoiding thinking about. I was really going to have to get on that. One of these days Jared was just going to drop by and I would be caught completely unprepared.

There was a knock on my door and it immediately opened. Dad was holding out the phone to me. "Cassie, it's Jared," he said.

I rolled my eyes closed and everything inside of me drooped. There was no telling my father to tell Jared I wasn't here. He had already heard my father say my name. Sometimes parents could be so clueless.

I took the phone and crossed my fingers. "Hey, Jared."

"Gracie! What's up?" he said, all chipper. "Where've you been."

"Oh . . . you know . . . around," I said, sitting on the edge of my bed.

My pulse was pounding in my ears. There was a long pause before he spoke again.

"Gracie, are you mad at me for some reason?" he asked finally.

"No!" I responded with a bit too much enthusiasm.

"Yes, you are. You're mad at me," he said with a sigh. "Why? Is it because of Christopher? Because I haven't even talked to him since the night of the dance. . . ."

The more he talked, the more my chest ached. He hadn't done anything wrong. It was me. All me. But I had a feeling he wouldn't like that explanation. I had to get him off the phone before I did something stupid like tell him to meet me at the lake for a swim and a hike to our special place. Then I'd be up all night and I'd sleep late tomorrow and the whole day would just be shot. I had resolved to concentrate on my work. I couldn't do this right now.

"I'm not mad, Jared, I swear," I told him, staring down at my knees. "I've just been really busy. There's so much to do around here right now and I have lessons and Lola and I have to train for the competition. . . ."

"I get it," Jared said. "But everyone needs to take a break once in a while, right? Why don't I come pick you up and—"

"I've had enough breaks," I blurted.

Ouch. That had come out sounding a bit more accusatory than I had intended.

"What does that mean?" Jared demanded. He sounded hurt.

"Nothing. Look, I'm sorry," I said, on the verge of tears. "I'm just really tired. I had a long day and this weekend is going to be crazy. I really just want to take a shower and go to sleep early. I'll talk to you soon. I promise."

"Okay, fine," Jared said tightly. "Sleep well, Gracie."

He hung up the phone and I burst into quiet tears. Why did he have to say something that sweet to me after I had spent the whole week dodging him? It just made me feel ten times worse. Clearly I had let everything get too complicated. I had always been a person who knew exactly what she wanted. Now I had no clue anymore.

You're just tired, I told myself, feeling pathetic as I pressed my pillow to my face. *Just get in the shower and relax. You'll feel much better.*

I got up, dried my tears, and grabbed my pajamas, already salivating for the feeling of my damp hair against the crisp, clean sheets. Everything would look brighter in the morning. It had to.

The next morning wasn't brighter, though. It was, in fact, downright dreary. Gray clouds crowded the sky and the air was thicker than oatmeal. It was one of those days when it didn't matter what I wore. Even if I walked around naked, my skin was going to be wet and sticky.

To add serious insult to injury, my first lesson of the morning was with the Locke boys. They had been behaving better of late, but for them that meant one step shy of Tasmanian devils. The good news was, if you chose to look at it that way, I had also agreed to take on all of

Penny's weekend lessons so that she could have a break. It was going to be a lot of work, but it would also get me a lot closer to the money I needed for my entry fee.

Hopefully, that thought would help get me through the insanity of the next two days.

Much to my surprise, the Locke boys were pretty tame that morning. It was as if the humidity had wilted the evil spirits right out of them. Josh sat quietly on the far side of the fence, ripping grass out of the ground next to the leg of the viewing bench while I led Seth around on Bubba, one of our larger horses. Seth, for once, wasn't bouncing up and down or squirming. With his little brow knit he actually looked like he was concentrating. Could it be?

"Seth, you're doing really well today," I said, feeling benevolent toward him for not torturing me. "Think you might want to try going around once on your own?"

"Really?" he asked, his face lighting up. Then he shrugged, as if remembering he was supposed to play it cool. "Okay."

"Do you remember what to do?" I asked.

"Yeah."

"Tell me," I said.

"To get him to go, I nudge him with my heels. To get him to stop, I pull back on the ropes and say 'whoa.'"

"Exactly. Except the ropes are called *reins*," I told him. "And if he starts to go too fast, you do the same thing, okay?"

"Okay."

I let Bubba's lead rein go and stepped into the center of the ring. Seth looked at me with uncertainty and I nodded. "Go ahead."

As soon as Seth and Bubba started moseying around on their own, Josh snapped to attention and came over to the fence to watch. Seth looked exhilarated and scared all at once as he made the first turn and rode Bubba down the long side of the paddock. He looked good up there, sitting lightly in the saddle, in complete control. I couldn't help grinning. Who knew that all this time when I had just been trying to tame these kids, they had actually learned something?

I heard a car pull into the driveway and I knew it was Jared even before he came into view. My heart took a nosedive and I didn't even look over my shoulder as he pulled up alongside the fence and stopped. I had to keep an eye on Seth. At least that was the excuse I was giving myself.

"Hey, Gracie," he said. He walked over to the fence behind me and hung his arms over the top rung.

I glanced at him over my shoulder. He looked perfectly happy and confident as always. As if no harsh words had been exchanged. He also looked completely model-worthy in a tight white T-shirt and battered brown cargo shorts.

"Hey," I replied. "What's up?"

"Got a minute?" he asked.

"Not really," I said, keeping one eye on Seth. "We're in the middle of a lesson."

Jared glanced at Seth as if noticing him for the first time. "Is that one of the crazy boys?"

"Shhh!" I chided him. "Yes."

Jared whistled. "Wow. You're like a lion tamer or something."

Seth and Bubba reached the point at which they had started their solo run and Seth brought Bubba to a stop perfectly. I really could have burst into ecstatic tears right there.

"Nice work, Seth!" I shouted.

"My turn! My turn!" Josh cried, jumping up and down.

"All right, Seth. Let's get you down and give Josh a try," I said.

"No! I wanna go again!" Seth whined.

"You have to give your brother a turn," I told him, crossing over to the horse's side.

"No! I'm good at it! He stinks!" Seth shouted.

"No I don't! You stink!" Josh shot back, pushing the gate open.

"Seth, come down," I said patiently. "We'll get you back up there before the end of the lesson."

"No! It's my horse!" Seth shouted, his eyes darkening as he clung to the reins. I knew their good behavior was too good to be true.

"Seth. Am I going to have to give you a time-out?" I asked.

"You can't give me a time-out!" he said. "You're not my mother."

Then he dug his heels into Bubba's side and Bubba lurched forward, heading straight for Josh.

"Seth, stop!" I said, grabbing for the lead rein. It was just out of my grasp. Josh was still running toward us, oblivious to danger. "Josh! Get back!" I cried, my heart in my throat. "No!"

Bubba was right on top of Josh. Seth screamed, clearly forgetting how to stop a horse in all the panic. And then, suddenly, I saw a flash of white and Jared had yanked Josh right out of the horse's path. I ran forward, grabbed Bubba's reins, and stopped him in his tracks. Seth instantly slid off the side of the saddle and into my arms, crying. Josh burst into tears as well, stunned and upset at seeing his big brother cry.

"All right, you're both all right," I said to Seth, placing him on the ground. I felt like I was about to throw up, but I ran my hand over his hair to try to soothe him. My heart pounded in my temples. "Let's take a break."

I wrangled everybody to the other side of the fence, leaving Bubba to roam. Jared placed Josh down on the bench next to the stable and Seth sat beside to him, looking forlorn. I ran to the office and got them both tissues and cups of Gatorade, my heart still racing over the close call. Once they were all settled, I finally turned to Jared.

"Thanks. I'm glad you were here," I said.

"It was no problem," Jared said. "I'm just happy they're all right."

"Yeah, except now I have to give them both a safety lecture," I said, sighing as I glanced at the boys over my shoulder. "Again."

"Or we could just get out of here," Jared said with a mischievous smile.

I blinked. "What do you mean?"

Jared pulled two tickets out of his back pocket and held them up. "They're for the amusement park at Lake George," he announced. "Christopher and I were supposed to go, but since we're currently not speaking . . . I thought you and I could go down there for the day, go on a few rides, eat junk food 'til we puke. I hear they have a new roller coaster that practically breaks the sound barrier. What do you think?"

"Uh . . . I think you should have called me first," I said. "I can't do it. I have lessons all day."

Jared's face fell, then creased with irritation. "But I did call. Last night. And all week. It didn't really seem like you wanted to talk to me then, so I just came over."

I sighed, feeling cornered. My tension level was already pretty high from our near miss, and now he was attacking me.

"Look, Jared, I'm sorry I've been unavailable this week, but I'm really busy. Especially today. I had to take on all Penny's lessons just so I could make the money I need for that entrance fee."

"The entrance fee? Still?" Jared said, opening his hands. "If that's all it is, don't worry about it. How much do you need? If I pay it, will you come with me today?"

He reached for his wallet and my mind, for a moment, went blank. Was he kidding me? He was just going to pay my five-hundred-dollar entrance fee so he could get me to go to Lake George?

"Jared, what are you doing?" I asked.

"I'm giving you money," Jared said, pulling out a few hundreds.

"Whoa," Seth said, staring at all that green.

"It's really not that big a deal," Jared said.

"It's a big deal to me!" I told him. "God!

You can't just throw money around to get your way. Not with me. What are you trying to do, *buy* my time?"

"No! You need the money and I'm giving it to you," he said. "At the end of the day you'll have the same amount of money, but you'll be having fun instead of baby-sitting brats."

"Hey!" Seth said. "We're not brats."

"Beg to differ," Jared said under his breath.

"I'm not taking your money," I said stoically. It was insulting, how it was nothing to him. How he could just throw it around, like he had that night at the country club, bribing that waiter for a reason that was still unexplained. The money I had been working for all summer was just sitting in his wallet and he was ready to just toss it away so he could go on his little amusement park trip. Who did he think he was?

He's a Kent, a little voice in my mind said. A voice that sounded a lot like my father's. Maybe Jared was finally showing his true colors.

His eyes flashed. "Why not?"

"Because I'm going to earn it myself," I told him. "That was the plan all along and that's what I'm going to do."

"Well, what am *I* supposed to do?" he asked. "You know, I decked my best friend for you and you're acting like I'm some kind of villain."

My jaw dropped. "I thought you did that because he was wrong, not to impress me."

"That's not what I mean," Jared said, his eyes flashing. "I just . . . God, Gracie! I just want to spend some time with you!"

"If that's the case, then you're just going to have to wait until the end of the weekend," I told him. "Sorry if that puts a cramp in your plans," I added sarcastically.

"Why are you being such a bitch about this?" he asked. "I'm just trying to help you out. What's wrong with helping you out so that we can both have a little fun?"

"Ooooo!" the boys said when they heard the word "bitch."

"I can't believe you just said that to me," I told him, crossing my arms over my chest. "You're just like your father, you know that? He waltzed right in here with his strip mall idea and when everyone didn't immediately bow down to him, he tried to buy the town's affections by offering to renovate the theater. Now you're just trying to buy me off."

"Like the Policastros didn't just jump at the chance to sell the rest of you out," Jared said.

I narrowed my eyes. He had no right to talk about Donna and Derek's parents that way. He didn't know them. He didn't know how much they loved that theater and how long they had hoped to bring it back to its former glory. As much as the rest of us loathed the idea of tearing down the orchard to put up stupid stores, I don't think anyone in town blamed the Policastros for taking Mr. Kent up on his offer. It was their dream come true.

Besides, we could still stop the development. Contrary to what Jared and his father clearly thought, the Kents could not always get their way.

"Well it's not over yet," I said. "This conversation, however, is."

I turned to Seth and Josh and held out my hands. "Come on, boys. We still have twenty minutes left."

I took them back into the paddock and saddled Josh up, pointedly keeping my back to Jared until I heard him stalk back to his car in a huff and speed off.

Chapter Twenty-two

The following night I abstained from going to the town planning board meeting with my parents, not in the mood for the drama — or for seeing Mr. Kent. I had abstained from pretty much everything all day, other than my morning lessons. Food? I barely had an appetite. Fun? When Donna had suggested spending the afternoon at the lake, just applying sunscreen had sounded like a huge pain. Conversation? I think all my parents had heard from me all day were the occasional grunts. My mind was elsewhere. All I could think about was my argument with Jared and every time I thought about it, I felt even more indignant.

I couldn't believe how easy it was for Jared to just write off five hundred dollars. Like I was being silly, thinking that was a large amount of money. I still felt irritated over the fact that he thought he could just waltz over to the ranch at any moment and I would be free to hang out with him. Like he was the only thing I had going on in my life. Please.

Finally, after my parents left for the meeting, I could no longer ignore my empty stomach. I grabbed the truck keys and headed for Pete's, suddenly craving one of Luke's greasy burgers. As a bonus, I knew the diner would be all but deserted, what with the entire town packing the town meeting room.

So when I walked in, I was surprised to see Derek there, sitting alone, munching on some fries.

"What are you doing here?" he asked.

"Moping. You?"

"Avoiding," Derek said as I plopped down across from him. "Donna's at the meeting with the 'rents. Any second I expect to see an angry mob with pitchforks driving them out of town."

"What can I get you, Cass?" Luke called out from behind the grill. It seemed even Elaine wasn't working tonight.

"Burger with the works and fries," I shouted back. "You mad at your dad?" I asked Derek, stealing a fry.

"Not really. I understand," he said, then smiled. "And he couldn't be more psyched about the renovation."

"That's good," I said, staring down at the table.

"What's the matter, Cass?" he asked. "I would have thought you'd be out with Jared tonight. Summer's almost over, right? Gotta get in the quality time," he joked.

"Please. I am so through with Jared Kent," I said, even though my heart ached.

"What? Why?" he asked.

"Let's just say he turned out to be more like his father than I thought," I told him as Luke deposited my burger in front of me.

"Really? Huh," Derek said, sounding surprised.

"What?"

"Well, a couple of weeks ago I would've said good riddance, but I was kind of getting the idea that he was different, too," he said with a shrug.

My chest tightened. "Why?"

"Did you know he called me after that day at the lake?" Derek said.

I nodded, the tightness intensifying. "He mentioned something about that."

"I thought that was pretty cool, you know? He didn't have to apologize for his idiot friends," Derek said. "And when I thought about it, I realized that while all those other jackasses were showing off and spouting about their trust funds, Jared had nothing to say. He doesn't seem to really put much stock in that crap. Not like the rest of them, anyway."

I swallowed hard and toyed with a French fry, not enjoying this new feeling of guilt that was sprouting up inside of me. "Yeah, but he offered to pay my entrance fee like it was nothing. Just so I'd go to Lake George with him."

"And you turned him down?" Derek blurted.

"Of course I did! I'm not his charity case," I said.

"Okay, you're right. Sorry," Derek said, chagrined. "But I doubt he was trying to throw his money in your face to make you feel bad. He probably just wanted to spend time with you.

And for that, I just have to commend him on his good taste," he added with a smirk.

I stared down at my burger, my appetite completely gone. Derek was defending Jared. *Derek* defending an *invader*. The more I thought about it, the more I realized he was right. All the other invaders loved to talk about how much their things cost or how big their houses were or how many cars they had in their many garages, but Jared wasn't like that. Since I had met him, he had never shown off about his wealth—not once.

Well, except for that first day when he had told me to get off his property. But really, he was well within his rights.

"I'm sure he just wanted to help," Derek said, taking a sip of his soda. "It's not his fault he was raised in a house where money was no object and was probably the solution to any and all problems."

I stared at Derek in wonder. "Do you realize that you almost sound enlightened? You. The number one invader-hater."

"Hey, I'm starting college in a few weeks. I'm trying to broaden my mind," he joked.

I got up, dropped some money on the table, and grabbed my bag, suddenly energized.

"Where're you going?" Derek asked.

"I have an invader to apologize to," I said, giving him a quick hug. "Thanks, D."

"Anytime, C."

I raced outside into the muggy night air and hopped into the pickup truck. It was almost eight P.M. but the sun was still sinking. I just hoped Jared had skipped the town meeting again. And that he was in a forgiving mood. My heart pounded like I had sucked down ten cups of coffee. Nerves were a freaky thing.

As I turned up Town Line Road I heard sirens in the distance and my nerves sizzled even hotter. Sirens were not a normal occurrence around Lake Logan. As the wailing grew louder, I said a quick mental prayer that nothing was on fire and no one had gotten hurt. Then I turned onto Murphy Street and slammed on the brakes, veering slightly off the road. An ambulance went flying by me in the opposite direction, lights flashing, siren deafening. Once it had turned the corner and was gone from sight I shakily turned the truck back onto the street. Now all the little hairs on my arms were standing on end. If the ambulance was coming from this direction, it was probably one of the invaders. All their houses were out this way.

I pressed down on the gas, sitting forward in my seat, drenched in foreboding. I had to see Jared. Now.

As I turned up his driveway, I tried to tell myself to chill. What were the chances that of all the invaders in this town, Jared had been the one in the back of that ambulance? I was being way too Donna-like. Everything was fine.

That was when the house came in to view, and I could see the red light from the top of a police car strobing against its white walls.

I pressed my foot into the brake and threw the truck into park, not trusting myself to drive any further. My entire body trembled.

Oh, God. Please let everyone be all right, I thought, my stomach clenching. *Please, please, please.*

Up ahead I saw Deputy Do-Right, whose real name was Doug Davis, walk out the front door of the house and share a few words with a woman in a maid's uniform. I practically fell out of the truck and jogged over to him on my weakened knees.

"Doug! Doug! What's going on?" I called out.

Doug squinted through the waning light. His thin mustache twitched and he removed his wide deputy's hat. "Cassandra Grace, is that you?"

"Yeah, it's me, Doug," I said impatiently. "You've known me since birth, all right? What's going on here? Is everyone all right?"

We were standing next to his police cruiser now and he opened the door, leaning his hands on top. "Well, now, I'm not sure I'm at liberty to tell you that."

I could have reached out and strangled him. Doug was two years older than me and I had once saved him from being beaten up on the playground by a couple of bullies by threatening to tell their parents. But ever since he had become a deputy, he loved to act like he had ultimate power in every situation.

"Doug, listen, the Kents are friends of mine," I said, trying to breathe. "If you don't tell me what's going on right now, I am going to go into town tomorrow and tell everyone about that time in third grade when my mom and I caught you walking to school with your underpants on the *outside*."

Doug's face went ashen. Clearly he had thought I had forgotten about that incident. Maybe living in a place where you knew everything about everyone wasn't *such* a bad thing.

"All right, fine," he said, slamming the door. "Robert Kent was on his way out to the town meeting and he had a heart attack."

The earth dropped out from under my feet. "What?" I heard myself gasp.

My mind reeled. Poor Jared! Poor Mrs. Kent! What they must have been going through just then!

"He's all right as of now. EMTs got here in time," Doug continued. "His family went with him to County Hospital. Now, they probably won't let anyone but family visit him. . . ."

But his warning fell on deaf ears. I had already turned around and strode purposely back to the truck. There was only one thing on my mind just then—Jared needed me. I had to get to him.

The nurse behind the emergency room desk looked me up and down with a scowl as I raced toward her. She pulled her aqua-colored sweater over her broad shoulders and smoothed it down.

"Hi, I'm looking for Robert Kent. I think he was just brought in a little while ago," I said, out of breath.

"Are you family?" she asked in a bored way. Couldn't she see I was panicking over here?

"No, but—"

"I can only give out information to family members. Sorry," she said, looking anything *but*.

"You don't understand," I told her, flattening my sweating palms on top of the high desk. "I just want to find out where I can find the family. Is there a waiting room?"

She sighed grandly. "I *told* you, I can't help you."

"Can't or won't?" I blurted, my eyes flashing.

"Look, I don't need your attitude," she snapped back.

"Attitude? *Attitude?*" I said, starting to unravel. "I am the last person on the planet who has *attitude*. You are the one giving me the attitude. Now I need to find my boyfriend and I need to find him *now*!"

The nurse blinked at me, impressed. But when she opened her mouth to reply, I had a feeling she was still going to blow me off.

"I'm right here," I heard Jared say.

I turned around and sure enough, there he was, walking toward me from a pair of double doors. His face looked pale, his hair was messed in a non-stylish way, and his eyes were rimmed in red. He enveloped me in his arms and hugged me so tight I heard something crack.

"Are you okay?" I asked him, pulling back. "I went over to your house and Doug told me that—"

"You were at my house?" Jared asked, his forehead creased as if he was trying very hard to concentrate. "Why?"

I wasn't prepared for that question. We were supposed to be talking about his father, not me.

"That's not important," I told him firmly. "How's your father?"

"He's an idiot," Jared said harshly.

He walked past me and sat down in one of the plastic emergency room chairs. He folded his arms over his chest and scowled at the floor, seeming so much like a petulant kindergartner that I suddenly knew exactly how he had looked at age five.

"Jared? What's going on?" I asked, sitting next to him.

He collapsed forward, let out a sigh, and covered his face with his hands. When he looked back over his shoulder at me, there were fresh tears in his eyes. "This is the whole reason we came up here," he said, leaning his elbows on his thighs as he hunched. "A couple months ago, back in the city, my father had a minor heart attack. His doctors told him he had to take a break and they suggested getting away for the summer. My mom knew all his business part- ners were going to be out in the Hamptons, so he would just be working, anyway, if we went there, so . . ."

"So you came up here instead," I finished.

Suddenly I remembered how old and almost frail his dad had looked at the town meeting. How Jared had pumped the gas that day when he hadn't known I was watching, and opened doors for his dad like a butler. This was the reason Jared had bribed that waiter at the Summer Fling. A man with a heart condition shouldn't have been ordering rare steak. Jared had just been trying to protect his father, who clearly had no interest in listening to doctor's orders.

No wonder Jared had never wanted to talk with me about the strip mall. No wonder he resented being here. His father had dragged him to Lake Logan because his doctor had told him to change his lifestyle, yet it sounded as if his father hadn't changed one bit.

"So we came up here instead," Jared repeated. He sat up straight, then slumped back in his chair, kicking his legs out. "Only about five seconds after we got here he came up with this strip mall idea, and then he's doing all this research and talking to developers, fighting with the town hall and your parents . . . on the phone with the state about the theater and the landmark thing. If anything, he's been just as stressed out up here as he was at home. It's like he's incapable of stopping. And now he's gone and given himself another freakin' heart attack," he finished angrily, throwing an arm toward the doors he had walked through.

My heart swelled with sorrow for him. I wrapped my arm around his back and huddled as close to him as I could get in the crappy, old-fashioned chairs.

"Jared, I am so sorry," I told him.

"When I walked through those doors and saw you talking back to that nurse, I swear I thought I was seeing things," Jared said. "You were really handling yourself there."

"Yeah, well, I wanted to find you," I said, swallowing back a lump in my throat. "I'm sorry about what happened yesterday. I've just had a lot going on. . . ."

The moment I said it, I felt like a heel. Clearly Jared had a lot more to worry about than I did.

"I understand. I don't think either one of us was exactly in the right," he said with a sigh. "I'm just glad you're here."

"Me, too," I told him truthfully.

The double doors opened and we both looked up to find his mother walking through them, looking harried. She had her cell phone in her hand as her eyes darted around the room.

"Mom!" Jared called out, standing. I stood with him, my heart freezing.

She looked somewhat relieved as she joined us. "They're taking him up to ICU to monitor him," she said. "He might need surgery, but they think he's going to be okay."

"Good," Jared said, looking more relieved than he sounded.

"Hello, Cassie," she said offhandedly. Almost as if she expected me to be there. "Listen, I'm going to call Doctor Burke. I don't want these people doing anything to your father without his approval."

"Okay. Good idea," Jared said with a nod.

"I'll be right outside," she said, pointing. "If you hear anything, come get me."

Jared nodded again and his mother weaved unsteadily through the maze of chairs toward the automatic doors. I watched her, my chest heavy, as she dialed her cell with shaking fingers. She hugged herself as she held the phone to her ear. It was obvious that she was distraught and scared. And standing outside, she looked very alone.

At that moment she ceased to be Susan

Morris-Kent, the woman who had broken my mother's heart. She ceased to be an obnoxious invader. She was just a woman who was petrified for her husband. At that moment, she was just a normal person. Just like anyone else.

I had left my parents a message letting them know what was going on, and my mom was waiting up for me with a cup of tea when I got home a few hours later. Once Robert was resting peacefully, the nurses managed to convince Jared and his mother that it was okay to head back to their house for some much-needed rest. Jared kissed me good-night at the car and told me he and his mother would probably be back at the hospital first thing in the morning. He had promised to keep me posted.

As I trudged into the kitchen, I had never felt so emotionally exhausted.

"Hey," my mother said sympathetically, getting up from her chair at the table. I practically collapsed into her arms. She kissed my forehead, then went to pour me some water from the kettle. "Everything okay?"

I pulled out a chair and plopped into it.

"They think he's going to be fine," I said. I traced a knot in the wooden table with my fingertip, thinking about Jared. He had been so angry. So sad. So scared. It wasn't fair that he had to handle all this himself—comforting his mother and making sure she was okay as well as his dad. I wished there was something more I could do for him.

"How's Jared doing?" my mother asked, returning to the table with a mug of steaming water. She ripped open a tea bag and placed it into the mug.

"He's all right," I said, toying with the tab on the tea bag. "Kind of angry, actually."

"I guess I could see that," my mother said, taking a sip of her tea. "And . . . Susan?" she asked tentatively.

I glanced up at her. I could tell it was taking a lot of effort for her to look me in the eye just then.

"I don't know," I told her truthfully. "She seems really scared. And kind of . . . alone."

My mother nodded and suddenly became very interested in her mug. "Well, I always assumed she must have really loved him," she said. "To do all the things she did."

"She does," I replied automatically. "I can definitely tell." My heart hurt, thinking of her and the way she had spent most of the night staring into space, chewing on her thumbnail. Every loud noise made her jump and whenever her cell phone vibrated, she ran out into the night like it was on fire.

"Mom?" I said, holding my breath. "Do you think you and Susan could ever . . ."

As soon as I started the sentence I wanted to take it back. I knew how much Jared's mother had hurt my mom. The woman had to have tons of friends who could come up here and be with her. I was sure it was the last thing on my mother's mind.

"What, honey?" she asked me gently.

"Nothing," I said, exhausted tears welling up behind my eyes. No matter what ever happened to us, I was never going to let anything come between me and Donna. For the rest of our lives, I was going to be there for her. I promised myself right then and there. I didn't want either one of us to ever have to go through something like this alone.

My mother sighed and shifted in her seat, leaning forward. "You know, I think it's about time I call my old friend Susan and see how she's doing."

I couldn't have been more surprised if my father had just walked in wearing an "I Heart Robert Kent" placard.

"Really?" I asked, my spirit soaring.

My mother smiled in a reassuring way. "Some things are more important than grudges," she said, reaching out to squeeze my hand.

I jumped out of my seat and hugged her like I had never hugged her before.

Chapter Twenty-three

*T*wo days later I sat at my desk, staring at the pile of cash in front of me, feeling like an utter failure. The county competition was in three days and I didn't have the money I needed. I was still a hundred dollars short.

How had I let it get this far? I had sabotaged myself right from the start of the summer. Now, thinking back, I could pinpoint five or six moments when I had made the wrong choice. Five or six moments in which, if I had made the responsible decision—if I had stayed home and done my work—everything would be different now. I would be happily stashing this money in an envelope for Saturday and heading out to the lake with Donna instead of sitting here feeling beyond depressed and disappointed in myself.

No regrets, I thought, pretending that my heart wasn't five times its normal weight. *You had a great summer. You got to know Jared. You had your first kiss. You had all kinds of fun and did some crazy things you never would have done before. Who knows? Maybe all that was worth four years of part-time jobs on top of school work.*

There was a light rap on my bedroom door and I jumped. If my parents saw the money and the entry form they were going to ask what was up. But they were going to find out sooner or later. May as well get it over with.

"Come in," I said, slumping. This was not going to be pretty.

I sat right up when Jared stepped into my bedroom. We had spoken a few times, but I hadn't laid eyes on him since that night in the hospital. He looked good. The stress was gone from his face and the color was back. Plus he was wearing this navy blue T-shirt that made his eyes look like the lake after a storm.

"Hey," he said with a smile.

"Hi." I was on my feet and in his arms. "How's your dad?"

"He's okay," he said. "They think he's okay, anyway."

"And your mom?" I asked.

"She's handling it," Jared said, pulling back. "It was really nice of your mom to come over, though. They were in the backyard for hours yesterday. I think it took her mind off things. For a while anyway."

I smiled, proud of my mom. She had been so emotionally spent when she got back from the Kents' the night before, she had gone right to bed without divulging any details. All she *had* told me was that she was glad she had taken the plunge.

Jared sat down on the edge of my bed and blew out a sigh. When he looked at me again, my heart thumped extra hard. I could tell by his expression that he had bad news. I lowered myself back down on my desk chair.

"Well, the good news is, my dad's dropping the strip mall plan," he said.

"What?"

"Yeah. He's not gonna be working for a while," Jared said, swallowing. "Don't worry, though, he had already started the ball rolling on the theater deal, so I guess it's a win-win for Lake Logan," he added with a wry little laugh.

"Okay, forget all that stuff," I said, waving a hand. I could process this news later. "What do you mean he's not gonna be working for a while? What's going on?"

Jared blew out a sigh. "His doctor back in the city wants him to stay on bed rest. He also wants to get him down there so he can observe him for a few days," he added. He paused, as if letting this information sink in. "We're leaving this afternoon."

"*Leaving* leaving?" I asked automatically. I knew the answer, though. The summer was almost over. There would be no point in the Kents going back to the city for a few days, then returning to Lake Logan for the last week or two.

"Yeah," Jared said quietly. "Leaving leaving."

I couldn't believe this was happening. This was the last time I would be in the same room with Jared. I felt so hollow inside I was surprised I could still breathe.

Jared leaned forward and pulled my hand toward him, holding my fingers lightly. "I don't want to go, but my parents need me right now."

"I know," I said, irritated to hear the tears in my voice. I trained my eyes on our intertwined hands.

"I'm gonna miss you, though," Jared said, ducking his head so he could look into my eyes. "This has been the best summer of my life, Gracie."

"Come on," I said, scoffing. "You've been to Europe. You've hung out in the Hamptons—"

"Best summer of my life," he repeated.

I smiled and a tear spilled down my cheek. I wiped it away quickly. Jared leaned in and kissed the exact spot where it had fallen. When he sat back again, I saw his gaze travel past my shoulder to the stack of money on my desk. I thought about swiping it into a drawer, but it was too late. He had already seen it.

"Is that the infamous entry fee?" he asked with a small smile.

"Sort of," I told him. I didn't care about it anymore. I didn't care about anything. All I wanted to do at that moment was curl up in a ball and sleep until college started. Maybe even longer. Everything was falling apart.

"What do you mean, sort of?" Jared asked, his brow creasing.

"I'm a hundred dollars short," I said with a sigh, slumping back.

"You're kidding. After all that?" Jared said.

"There wasn't as much 'that' as you think," I told him. "I didn't actually work much this summer, when it comes down to it."

Jared considered me for a moment. "I almost hate to suggest this . . . ," he said.

"Don't," I told him. "You're not paying for it."

"This isn't a buy-off, Gracie. Come on. It's my fault you don't have that money. We both know it," he said, his eyes pleading. "If I had never shown up here this summer, you'd probably have twice what you need."

I said nothing. He wasn't wrong.

"So let me give you the hundred," he said. "You did teach me how to ride this summer, right? Consider it a fee."

I smirked. "You didn't need much of a lesson. I think you were born to be on a horse."

"Well, my impressive natural abilities aside," he said with false modesty. "What do you think? Will you let me help you? Please, Gracie."

I felt a little thrill of excitement trying to expel the bleakness inside as I looked into his eyes. I could do this. I could still enter the competition. This summer didn't have to go down as a total waste. Jared smiled hopefully. He so clearly wanted to do this for me, and this time, it didn't feel like an insult or a bribe. Jared would get nothing out of it but the satisfaction of giving me something I wanted. It felt like a gift, and I caved.

"Okay, fine," I said finally.

"Yes!" Jared said, reaching for his wallet. He slipped two fifty-dollar bills out and handed them over. "Now I expect you to win," he told me with a grin.

"I'll do my best," I said. "Thank you," I added, looking him in the eye. "This means a lot to me."

"It means a lot to me that you took it," Jared said. He glanced at his watch and stood. "I should get going," he said reluctantly.

I stood as well, tucking the money into my

pocket. "I can't believe you're going."

"I know. Sort of feels wrong," Jared said, glancing around. "Two months and, I don't know, this place kind of grows on you."

My heart was pounding painfully and my eyes stung with tears, but I didn't want to cry. I didn't want to make this a big dramatic scene. Jared and I had spent a great summer together, but I wasn't kidding myself. I was off to Vermont in a couple of weeks. He was going back to the city and Columbia. Back to his friends and his parties and his celebrity elbow-rubbing. I knew that he loved me, but how long was that going to last once he was gone?

"So," he said.

"So," I replied, taking a deep breath. "I'll . . . I'll call you and let you know how Lola and I do."

Jared blinked, surprised. "Oh, I'll talk to you before then," he said. "I'll call you from the car on the way back to the city. I'll call you so much you'll be sick of me."

I smiled. "Not possible."

Jared reached out and cupped my face with his hands, tilting my head up. "I know what you're thinking, Gracie. You think I'm going to go back to the city and get back with my friends and forget all about this summer, but that's not going to happen."

"No?" I asked. It was pretty much the only thing I could say without crying.

"Don't you get it yet? I love you, Cassandra Grace," he told me.

Everything inside of me ached. It took every ounce of strength I had to keep from bursting into tears. I didn't want him to go. I felt like if he did, I wouldn't even be able to breathe anymore.

I took a deep breath, squeezed my eyes closed, and decided that one more risk would be well worth it.

"I love you, too," I blurted. And it felt good. *Really* good.

Jared tipped his head back. "Finally!"

I laughed, but he stopped it short with a kiss. For the first time there was an urgency in the way he kissed me. The languid, lazy moments of summer were gone. Now he was kissing me like he, too, was afraid to let go.

"I'll talk to you before you know it," he said when we parted.

"Okay," I said with a nod. "I love you."

"Can't stop saying it *now*, can ya?" he joked, his voice husky.

"Apparently not," I replied with a grin.

He kissed me one more time and hit me with a killer smile as he headed for the door. "Bye," he said.

"Bye," I replied.

He stepped out, closed the door behind him and was gone.

I collapsed back on my bed, my breath short and shallow. I ached to run after him and make the whole thing last for at least a little while longer, but I stayed where I was. The realistic side of me knew that it really was quite possible that I had just seen Jared for the last time, whatever his intentions were right now. And if that was the case, I wanted to remember that perfect kiss as our last. I wanted to remember him here in my room, telling me he loved me — telling me I loved him back.

It might not have been the daring thing to do, but it was the Cassie thing to do. And it was time for me to get back to being me.

Chapter Twenty-four

"I can't believe you're late. You're never late," Donna said to me as I turned onto the fairgrounds on Saturday morning. Lola's trailer bumped loudly as I hurtled through the gate. "Well, you know, except for that one time when you dissed me for Jared. . . ."

"That's great, D. Rub it in. That is *so* what I need right now," I said, my palms sweating as I gripped the steering wheel. I scanned the area, looking at the handwritten signs for some indication of the registration tent for the equestrian competitions. "Do you want me to remind you that this is all your fault?"

"Ugh! So not true! It was Derek," she replied, glaring at her brother, who was squeezed between her and the door.

"I tried to wake you up a *dozen* times!" he replied, pressing one hand to the ceiling as I navigated a turn rather quickly.

"Yeah. Likely story," she grumbled.

"Okay, there it is," I said. I turned the truck and parked next to a bunch of empty trucks and trailers. "I have about two minutes to get this entry fee over there," I said, grabbing my backpack. "You guys get Lola out of the trailer and bring her over to the inspection tent, okay?"

"You got it, babe," Donna said. She took out a mirror and checked her lipstick.

"Donna!" I shouted, getting out and slamming the door.

"I got her, I got her," Derek said, rolling his eyes. "Just go!"

I turned around and raced past the sign for the registration desk. A big red arrow pointed straight ahead. I hightailed it through a wide open stable to the far end where another arrow pointed me to the right. After taking the corner I paused, out of breath, and scanned the area. All I saw in front of me were dozens of pens holding pigs and goats and sheep for the livestock competitions. Where the heck were they sending me?

"Excuse me?" I said, stopping a tall cowboy in his tracks. "Where's the registration for the jumper competition?"

He lifted his chin and pointed. "See that tent over there?"

"That one?" I asked. It was a speck in the distance.

"Yep. That's the one."

"Thanks."

Suddenly I found myself wishing that I had joined the track team four years ago when my gym teacher had tried to recruit me. I turned on the speed as much as possible and sprinted clear across the field, side-stepping kids with balloons and a pack of guys my age, strolling along with a portable stereo. I almost took out a father with a toddler on his shoulders when he side-stepped in front of me and shouted a breathless apology as I kept running. Finally I slid to a stop in front of a table marked "Registration." The older woman behind it was clipping papers together and piling them into boxes. This did not look good.

"Excuse me," I said, gasping for breath. I fumbled in my bag for the envelope holding my fee and entry papers. "Is this where I register for the jumper competition?'

The woman turned her back to me to continue her work. Her white hair was curled so tightly it looked like the wool on some of sheep I had blown by a minute ago.

"Registration's closed," she said without looking at me.

"What? No!" I wailed. "I'm, like, a minute late."

"Exactly," the woman said, pushing her glasses up on her nose as she inspected a paper in front of her.

"But—"

"You had plenty of time to register yourself and your horse this morning during the allotted registration period," the woman said firmly, giving me a prissy look. "We do not set these rules for our own amusement. We set them to maintain order."

My heart sunk and I felt a familiar heat crawling up my neck. I felt like a five-year-old being admonished by my kindergarten teacher.

"Good day," the woman said.

"Yeah," I replied, turning away. I felt like I had swallowed a glass of acid. My throat and stomach burned with humiliation. I looked down at the envelope in my hands and paused, thinking of Jared. He would kill me if he saw me right now. I had stood up to Mrs. Locke. I had talked back to that nurse at the hospital. I had learned firsthand that I could do it. Was I really going to back down now and let something that meant so much to me just pass me by?

"No," I said aloud.

"Pardon me?" the woman said, surprised.

I turned around, my pulse racing, and stepped toward her again. A younger man in a blue sports jacket was checking out some of the papers and he looked at me with interest as well.

"Look, I know all about rules," I told her. "I've lived by them every single day of my life. But I also know that rules can be bent now and then and I'm asking you to do that for me. I worked hard to get here and so did my horse and I *need* to be in this competition. If your watch happened to be two minutes slow, I would have been on time. Please. Please, just take my entry fee. I mean, it's money, right? A lot of money. You can't just turn it down."

The man laughed and the woman eyed me with a sour expression.

"Actually, Deanne," the man said, glancing at his gold wristwatch. "I've got five minutes to nine."

I grinned at him, my heart skipping a hopeful beat. Deanne finally rolled her eyes and snapped her hand toward me.

"Hand it over," she said.

"Yes! Thank you. Thank you *so* much," I gushed, shakily pulling out the money and the entry form. "And thank you, Mr. . . ."

"I'm Richard Ryan," he said, shaking my hand. "I'll be announcing your competition."

"Cassie Grace," I said.

"Well, good luck, Cassie Grace," he said. "You have that much spunk out on the course and I have no doubt I'll be announcing you the winner."

"Thanks," I said, a thrill running straight through me.

Deanne handed me a numbered ribbon, a

receipt, and a copy of my form. "Bring this to the inspection site."

"I will," I said. "And thanks again. Really. You made my day."

She simply snorted and I turned around, elated and pretty much inflated by pride. I almost tripped myself when I saw Jared standing about five feet in front of me.

"Gracie, Gracie, Gracie," he said, shaking his head as he walked toward me. "I believe I created a monster."

"Omigod! What are you doing here?" I cried, throwing myself into his arms.

"What do you think I'm doing here?" he asked, hugging me tightly and lifting me off my feet. "All I heard about all summer was this competition. You really think I'd miss it?"

I looked up at him wide-eyed as he replaced me on the ground. "This is the best surprise ever."

He leaned down and kissed me and I felt like I would melt right there on the spot. A few days ago I thought I might never see him again. But here he was already. Right back in my arms.

"Come on," he said, wrapping his arm

around my shoulders. "I don't want you to be late for anything else. You need to get out there and make good on my investment."

"Oh, I will," I said giddily as we crossed the field again. "Suddenly I feel like kicking a little butt."

As Lola and I cleared the last water jump, I heard Jared, Donna and Derek, and my parents hollering for me from the stands. With each progressive jump the crowd grew a little more boisterous and I could feel Lola's adrenaline pumping as much as I could my own. She knew how well she was doing. Seven jumps down, one to go and we had cleared each one of them cleanly.

We turned and headed for the final fence. A hush fell over the crowd. The digital clock in the corner clicked away, timing our progress. We were going to come in under. No time faults. No touch faults. There was nothing between me and that grand prize but one more jump.

"Okay, Lola," I whispered. "This one's for all the carrots."

We launched into the air and I knew we had

it. I just knew. The crowd went crazy. Donna and Derek whistled. Jared shouted my name at the top of his lungs. As Lola's hooves reconnected with the ground, I felt light, elated, inflated. Everything that had happened this summer—all that work, all that play, all that risk-taking—all of it had led up to this moment. And it was all worth it. We crossed the finish line and I turned Lola toward the stands and caught Jared's eye. He was on his feet, applauding, and he tossed me a quick wink.

"I love you, Gracie!" he shouted, cupping his hands around his mouth.

Everyone near him laughed. There were still a few competitors to go, but as Lola and I cantered around toward the gate, I couldn't wipe the silly grin off my face. No matter what happened next, I felt like I had already won.

Don't ride off into the sunset yet! More summer romance awaits . . .

THRILL RIDE
by RACHEL HAWTHORNE

Megan has the coolest summer job ever, working—and living!—at a big amusement park. But it means three months away from her boyfriend . . . and three months *with* a really hot coworker. Talk about a roller coaster!

SUMMER IN THE CITY
by ELIZABETH CHANDLER

Jamie loves sports and she always falls for jocks—who turn out to be jerks. But this summer she'll be in a big city, with lots of sophisticated guys. And, uh oh . . . one very adorable lacrosse coach.

Thrill Ride

by RACHEL HAWTHORNE

I took my phone out of my backpack, looked at the number, and smiled. My sister. I flipped it open. "Hey, Sarah!"

She groaned melodramatically. "Are you ready to come home?"

I laughed. "I just got unpacked. Too late now!"

"So what's it like?"

"I've been here only an hour, but first impressions? It's going to be totally cool." I didn't want to tell her my doubts about my roommate. Otherwise she'd start hounding me to come home. She was almost as thrilled as Nick about my coming here. According to her, I'd abandoned her in her hour of need.

"Mom is driving me absolutely crazy," she said.

"Why do you think I took this job way up here?"

"The latest is that Mom thinks my wedding dress is too daring for church."

The neckline *was* low.

"Do you have to get married in church?"

"Why didn't you say something about the neckline when I was ordering it?" she asked.

"Number one, you were looking in a three-way mirror, so I figured *you* could see that half your boobs were showing, and number two, because it's your wedding. You should wear what you want."

"Half my chest isn't exposed."

"Almost."

"Shoot. I hate for Mom to be right."

I smiled. That was part of the reason that so much yelling was going on at the house right now. Mom and Sarah are both stubborn, convinced that her way is the only way.

"So what are you going to do?" I asked.

"Guess I'll see about changing out the gown, except that my one and only sister abandoned me for Canada—"

"I'm not in Canada."

"You might as well be. Just cross the lake and you're there."

"Do you have any idea how big Lake Erie is? It's like looking out on an ocean. You can't see the other shore."

"How can I go shopping for a gown without you to help me make a selection? You're my maid of honor. Maybe you could fly home for the weekend."

I laughed. "Sarah, I had to sign a blood oath that I would ask for only one weekend off all summer. And I plan to take it when you get married."

"That sucks. I never thought I'd say this, but I miss you, Megan. So what's it really like there?"

"I'm not sure yet. Ask me tomorrow."

"Okay. I gotta go. Love ya."

"You, too."

I hung up. I sometimes thought that the reason that Mom and Sarah fought so often was because they were so much alike. Headstrong, determined, bossy. I was more like Dad: laid-back, quiet, didn't let too much bother me. Which was the reason that I'd thought I wouldn't have much trouble adjusting to living with someone I didn't know.

And maybe Jordan wasn't that bad. I mean, she'd realized that she needed to pick up her mess and she'd done it . . . almost. It could work between us.

I went back to unpacking. I didn't have that much. My clothes went into the closet or in the dresser beside my bed. My toiletries went into the bathroom. I didn't think our suitemates were slobs, but four girls, two sinks, one counter did make for a lot of clutter. My laptop went on my desk where the DSL connection would keep me connected to the world. I put a few odds and ends on shelves nailed to the wall over my desk and placed my alarm clock on my desk next to the computer so it was near my bed for easy reach.

I looked at my watch. It was already seven. The sun was setting. I thought about calling Nick, but I guess I was being a little stubborn, hoping he'd call me.

This was insane. I grabbed my phone, slipped it into the pocket of my cargo shorts, along with my key, and headed out the door.

Outside I sat down on the sand, drew my legs up to my chest, and wrapped my arms around my knees. I hadn't expected to be homesick after just one day.

I took my cell phone out of my pocket and willed it to ring. Now I was being as stubborn as my sister, but I guess the truth was, Nick had hurt my feelings a little bit.

"This sucks big time," he'd said last night.

We were sitting in his car in my driveway. He'd taken me to dinner at Outback to celebrate my birthday.

"Let's not say good-bye tonight," I said. "Take me to the airport in the morning."

"Why? It's just putting off the inevitable."

"But it's more romantic at an airport."

"I don't see how. I wouldn't be able to go to the gate with you because of all the security stuff. We'd have to say good-bye outside the metal detectors. What's romantic about that?"

I'd sighed. "Well, then, I guess we'll say good-bye now."

"Yeah." He'd put his arm around me, drew me up against his side. "I'm sorry, Megan. It's just that I had plans for this summer."

I angled my face for easier access and kissed him. His arms tightened around me.

"God, I'm going to miss you, Megan. I don't know how I'll survive."

That's what a girl wanted to hear. Deep devotion. But it was only three months, and not all at once. I'd be back halfway through the summer for the wedding. And didn't absence make the heart grow fonder?

"Do you have to go?"

"You know I do. I gave them my word."

And that's when he started to sulk. It suddenly got really cold in the car, a drop in temperature that had nothing to do with the air surrounding us, and it frightened me a little to think that I might lose him, but it also frightened me to think that I was making my decisions based on what was best for Nick, rather than what was best for me.

"Nick, it's only for the summer."

"You don't even act like you're going to miss me."

"Of course I'm going to miss you."

I was already missing him. It was like he'd gone away from the moment I'd first told him about my summer plans.

Maybe that's the reason I was now sitting

on the shores of Lake Erie feeling lonely. We hadn't kissed good-bye. We'd barely *said* good-bye.

This was supposed to be a fun, exciting excursion. I didn't want to feel guilty about being here.

Bad news. I did.

Summer in the City

by Elizabeth Chandler

Jamie,
I'm signing books. Look for the pink
flamingo on The Avenue. My table
is in front of Hometown Girl.
Love, Mom

She had attached a festival map and circled her location. Before dealing with the fuss my mother always made when she first saw me, I decided to explore the place where she had chosen to live out her dream.

Some of the crowd that swarmed the closed-off blocks of Hampden's main street were dressed for heat and humidity. But there was a guy in a red, rhinestone-decorated Elvis outfit and women of all ages with huge, teased-out hair—beehives. The beehive ladies wore cat's-eye glasses, red lipstick, and stretchy print pants. Nearly all of the women and girls carried fantastic purses. They were "Baltimore Hons"—I realized, after reading a festival poster with photos from last year's Best Hon contest. My mother had said the festival celebrated working-class women and life in the 50s, a period which, apparently, had lasted a very long time in Hampden.

I bought a large sparkly clip from a booth and pulled my hair up in a loose ponytail, then purchased a bright pink boa. It was too light to make me hot and felt very girly as it drifted around my shoulders. *Maybe this was my summer to try out* really *girly,* I thought, as I worked my way down the Avenue, carefully circumventing the area where my mother would be signing books.

I was just starting to get hungry when I came upon a parked bus painted to look like a monstrous blue can of Spam. I lost my appetite when I realized people were standing around eating Spam burgers. Next to the bus, kids were bowling, rolling small balls down an alley, trying to knock over stacked cans of Spam. I felt as if I had landed on an alien planet.

But then I saw a group of great-looking

guys waiting for their chance to bowl, wolfing down the disgusting burgers, laughing and joking and being loud. With them was a Baltimore Hon, a girl as tall as I—check that, a guy! I saw it by the way he wobbled on his high-heeled mules as he crumpled up his drink cup and strode toward a trash can. I watched, smiling to myself, and at that moment, he became aware of me studying him and turned to look back.

I couldn't see his eyes—his green rhinestone sunglasses hid them—but he stared at me as if *I* were the one in drag as a Baltimore Hon. My eyes dropped to his stretchy leopard-print pants, which clung to extremely muscular legs. His feet were stuffed awkwardly into pink mules with fluffy toe pieces. I started to laugh, but he didn't. He just stared at me, so long that I turned to see if someone else, like Fat Elvis, was standing behind me. There was no one.

Feeling flirty and free in this city where I knew no one and no one knew me, I smiled and waved the end of my boa. I felt giddy with girl power, as if I had cast a spell on this guy who couldn't stop staring at me. He suddenly came to his senses, turned and walked on, but his eyes — his sunglasses — strayed back to me.

"Hey, hon, watch where you're going!" one of his friends yelled, but the guy had his eyes on me. He tripped over the street curb. Trying to catch his balance, unsteady on his high heels, he staggered wildly, then sprawled across the pavement. When he sat up next to the trash can, his red beehive wig sat cockeyed on his head. He snatched up his sunglasses, shoving them back on his face as if to keep people from recognizing him. His friends howled with laughter. The guy whirled around and hurled both fluffy pink shoes at them, realizing too late that it made him look like a girl throwing a hissy fit. Now his friends roared louder and others joined in.

The guy grabbed up his boa with a fierceness that made a flurry of feathers. I pressed the back of my hand against my mouth, but I was shaking with laughter. A big satin rose had tumbled out of his wig, and when he bent over in his leopard pants to retrieve it, it wasn't a pretty sight. A second rose that had been catapulted from his wig had rolled toward me. I picked it up, but the guy was obviously avoiding further glances in my direction, and I wasn't sure what to do with it.

"Excuse me," I called softly, as if it were possible to get his attention only.

His friends grinned at me—leered may have been a more accurate word. They realized that I was the one who had distracted him.

"Hi, hon," one of them called to me. "What's your name?"

Now I became self-conscious and was no more willing than the guy-Hon to cross the twenty-five feet between us.

"Look, your little sweetie has your rose," one of his friends told him.

Despite the guy's tan, I could see his cheeks coloring. Mine burned as well—"*little sweetie*"—what was that supposed to mean! The guys had that cocky jock look and were eyeing my extra long legs in an obvious, obnoxious way.

The Hon glanced over at me. I threw the rose at him like a strike through the heart of home plate, then hurried off in the opposite direction.

"Baby!" my mother greeted me.

"Hey, Mom."

"Everyone, this is my baby, Jamie. Isn't she beautiful?"

"*Very* beautiful," said the man sitting next to my mother at the signing table.

"Jamie, this is Viktor."

Light-haired, blue-eyed, and thirty–something, Viktor rose to shake my hand. Whoa, I thought, is this what romance publishers look like? Then I remembered: Mom called her editor Priscilla.

"It's a pleasure to meet you," Viktor said, in an accent that I thought was Swedish. He had a body perfect for modeling skimpy gym wear. Maybe he did publicity for the chick lit line, I thought—clever marketing!

"I've got a half hour more here, baby. Would you like the house key?"

"No, I'll get something to eat and hang out."

I left Mom to her fans, but when I was about thirty feet away, I turned back to look at her, trying to see her the way a stranger would. We had the same eyes, green, and the same hair, although hers, dyed now, was a paler yellow than my streaky blond. Standing just five foot five and sporting some big curves, wearing her hair and bangs too long for a woman who was fifty, she looked like a country western singer — or a romance writer, I reminded myself. I watched a woman clutching one of Mom's books to her breast, talking animatedly. Mom was radiant — she had found her dream.

I found a booth selling crab cakes, and carried my sandwich and iced tea to an area in front of the festival's main stage, choosing a seat in the last row. Up front, members of a school band with a color guard were wiping sweat off their faces. Hons of all ages were gathering, some of them practicing their poses, getting ready for the big contest. I scanned the group for my guy-Hon, but he wasn't there.

By the time I finished the crab cake, the heat and long drive from Michigan had caught up with me. Feeling pleasantly sleepy, I shut my eyes, soaking up the June sunlight, and thought about "my" Hon. Since he obviously wasn't enjoying his day in drag, I figured he was being initiated into some group. I wondered what he looked like without the wig and make-up, what kinds of things he liked to do, what his voice sounded like.

"You're desperate, Jamie," I told myself, "when you have romantic thoughts about a guy in high heels." Still, I tried to imagine what would make him smile and how his laughter sounded . . .

I woke up with a start, awakened by a clash of symbols during the National Anthem. Realizing that I was the only one sitting, I rose hastily to my feet. Something rolled off my lap. I picked up a pink satin rose, the one I had thrown back at my Hon. Quickly I looked around, but he was nowhere in sight.

I studied the rose, then attached it to my shirt, wrapping its wire base around my strap. The rose was old, which made it seem as if it had once been special to someone. I touched its fabric gently, lovingly. Dropping it in my lap was the most romantic thing a guy had ever done for me.